"THERE WAS MUCH

in our situation that reminded me of Columbus. We were crossing a great ocean, from east to west. A new world—a continent untouched by what passed for civilization on Attica—was waiting for us. No one else had ever made the crossing and returned (though three previous ships had made the attempt). And the crew were restless . . . perhaps incipiently mutinous."

The main human colony had survived . . . but barely, and unless some sort of new life was injected, would surely fail. Out there across the vast ocean an offshoot human colony had been planted—and none had heard from them. But the legend persisted that the others had succeeded. But, if so, how?

So the *Daedalus* expedition set out to sail the ocean in simple ships. For despite their starship and their science, they had no other means on the surface save those that had served the ancient navigators of Earth. So they sailed on . . . to mystery, to danger, to possible disaster for themselves and for that world.

BALANCE
OF
POWER

———◦———

Brian M. Stableford

DAW BOOKS, INC.
DONALD A. WOLLHEIM, PUBLISHER

1301 Avenue of the Americas
New York, N.Y.   10019

FIRST PRINTING, JANUARY 1979

1 2 3 4 5 6 7 8 9

PRINTED IN U.S.A.

1

Night fell swiftly, darkness consuming the sky as the sun's vestigial halo faded in the west. One of the crewmen moved slowly around the deck, lighting the lamps which hung head-high on the masts and the roof of the fo'c'sle. Lamps were lit in the cabins, too, and they cast weak orange beams from the portholes to catch the sheen on the long trailers of weed that bobbed in the bow-waves of the ship.

It was four days now since we had come once again into weed-infested sea. We were more than a hundred days out, and should be very near now to the coast of the western continent. Our closeness seemed to exaggerate the slowness with which we made headway. Day by day we pushed laboriously forward into the wind, which seemed to be trying to drive us away. Even a Columbus might have lost patience with it and allowed himself to be carried home, with the wind making his retreat easy. But we had one advantage that Columbus hadn't had: good maps. Slow though our progress was we could always measure it out, plotting our position with precision on a map that assured us that there *was* a destination to be reached, and that we were getting there.

With that exception laid aside, there was much in our situation that reminded me of Columbus. We were crossing a great ocean, from east to west. A new world—a continent untouched by what passed for civilization on Attica—was waiting for us. No one else had ever made the crossing and returned (though three previous ships had made the attempt). And the crew was restless . . . perhaps incipiently mutinous.

I stood in the bow of the ship looking down at the waves cut out from the water as we sliced our way through the loose weed. The waves were slow, and died quickly in the viscous water. The stars were out, and their reflected glow competed with a faint bluish bioluminescence. There was something slightly eerie about the impression it made. No doubt even that would be added to the crew's catalogue of complaint and unease.

We had had difficulty recruiting for the voyage. The arrival of the *Daedalus* on Attica had assured the *New Hope* a better chance than any of her predecessors, if only because of the food concentrates we were able to manufacture for her supplies (immodestly, I also rated my own presence something of a plus, but I'll not insist upon the point). Despite this, however, volunteers for the epic journey had been thin on the ground. The fishermen of the colony saw no real merit in exploration for the sake of exploration. They had work to do and families to keep, and that was as far as their personal horizons extended. The colony—which had taken its name, Lambda, from the continent on which it had been established (which took it, in turn, from the Greek letter which it vaguely resembled on the map)—was not an outstanding success. Life had been hard in the hundred-and-some years since the landing, and there was a very powerful ethic in force demanding hard work and the responsibility of each household to look after its own. There was little reward, in terms of social approval, for anyone willing to give up his work and home for a journey across the ocean that would take half a year at the least.

Nieland—the architect of the project and the designer of the ship—had ultimately managed to sign on a full complement of men, but they were not the men he (or any sane man) would have chosen. They had always worked with an ill grace, and found new excuses for grumbling day by day. They had come close to making the voyage intolerable, for themselves and for us.

It would not have been a happy trip anyhow. For days after we set out I had been very sick thanks to the interminable rolling of the boat—and so had many of the sailors. They were used to small fishing smacks, for the most part—we had only half a dozen trawlermen—and found the *New Hope* almost as alien as I did. Mariel had suffered too—perhaps more than I, though the way I had felt at the time seemed to preclude such a possibility.

Nieland, too, had been troubled. On regaining our health we three, and Nieland's companion Ling, had also recovered our good spirits. Not so the crew. The boredom of the long days had reinforced their sense of pointlessness. The further we drew away from Lambda the greater grew their superstitious fears. Three ships lost over the last hundred years . . . such ventures as this one condemned by fate . . . .

And the prevailing wind in our face, all the way. We had had no more than seven good days, with fair winds assisting us, and those had been offset by more than the same number of days when storm and tempest made progress impossible. I had been frightened then, to hear the timbers groaning in apparent desperation. There could be no greater contrast than between the ship that had brought us through hyperspace to Attica and the primitive three-masted schooner that was now carrying us over its ocean. On stormy nights I spent a great deal of time cursing the parsimony of the colony's administrators, who had refused the plan to build a steamship on the grounds that the energy-expenditure envisaged was too high.

Somewhere behind me, a bell rang four times. To the crew, that signaled that we were two hours into the watch. To me, it meant that it was time for the evening meal. I pulled myself away from hypnotic contemplation of the sea's sparkling surface and made my way below.

As always, the table in Nieland's cabin was set for five. I say "set," though there was little enough setting. We had been on a diet of pure concentrates for some time, as the ship's supplies of more substantial nourishment had dwindled away. We had a good deal in hand in terms of calorific values and essential vitamins, but our digestive tracts were misbehaving a little because of the absence of roughage. I was used to it, but for some it was merely one more excuse to be embittered. One of the some was our noble captain, whose name was Ogburn—a tall, big-boned man who suffered from a slight speech impediment and was angrily economical with his words. He contributed little to our post-prandial conversations, and cast something of a pall over the meals themselves, but his presence was necessary, for diplomatic reasons.

Nieland and Ling, representatives of Lambda's civil service (parasites, as some of the crew described them), provided an odd contrast. Nieland was short but very stocky, and had a tendency to the lugubrious. Ling was tall, slender and quick to smile, though his smile seemed to be quite synthetic and meaningless. It appeared like magic, and disappeared with rapid discretion, as I came into the cabin. Nieland merely nodded. Ogburn, whose back was to the door (in case he had to make a hasty exit) didn't look round.

I took my place beside Mariel, and began peeling the foil back from the pack of concentrates without further ceremony.

"We should reach land tomorrow or the day after," announced Nieland. He kept an overscrupulous check on our progress, measuring our position three or four times a day with the instruments that were his pride and joy.

"We've had no trouble with the weed so far," added Ling. "It doesn't seem likely that it will provide any significant hazard."

"Wind won't change," contributed Ogburn.

I took up my mug of Lambda's answer to instant coffee, and swilled down the first lumpy mouthfuls of concentrate.

"Why not station a couple of men with fishing lines tonight?" I said. "It's been four days now since we hit the weed—there ought to be plenty of fish about and we aren't making such headway that the lines would get torn or tangled."

Nieland shook his head. "It isn't a good idea to advertise the fact that we aren't making enough headway to lose a fishing line. And we'll hit solid weed soon, now. We can fish to our heart's content when we reach the shore."

I shrugged. Mariel ate silently, her eyes fixed on a knot of wood that stood up from the grain of the table about eight centimeters in from the edge. She was disturbed by the mood of the crew. She was also impatient—this was, basically, her trip. We had expected to find, on landing, that the Lambda colony had already established some kind of base on the western continent (named Delta for an even vaguer resemblance of shape), or at least that

8

they had a sufficiency of ships capable of making the journey. But we had found a colony in bad trouble, with the *New Hope* under construction and generating much ill-will as Nieland and his supporters were charged with misusing resources. Mariel had been disappointed, in that the indigenous inhabitants of Attica, who lived only on Delta, were the most nearly human and the most "advanced" of the three alien races with whom she was supposed to make contact during the mission. She had enjoyed a modest success with respect to the Salamen of Wildeblood—but they, as an amphibious species, had been somewhat remote from humanity. The Atticans were better approximations of primates, though slightly catlike in appearance. There had seemed to be much better prospects for establishing amicable relations between man and alien on Attica—mutually beneficial relations, too. But Mariel arrived to find that no avenues of communication had been opened up, and that there was no intercontinental traffic of any kind. Not only would she have to work from scratch, but there was hardly time for anything more than a brief expedition to Delta which might not even result in a fruitful contact being made. So far, she had found Attica a sad disappointment.

"There are birds sleeping in the rigging tonight," said Ling, changing the subject. "They're relying on us to carry them back to shore. That's a good sign."

Privately, I thought: *Yes, but if anything should happen, they still have their wings.* I did not, of course, voice any such thought. Nor did anyone else. But I didn't need Mariel's talent for reading minds to know that there were certain disturbing thoughts lurking furtively in the minds of my companions. We were two days from shore, and it had not been too difficult so far. But three other ships had made this journey, and not one had returned. They had been designed as well as the *New Hope,* built as strong. One, or even two, might have found exceptionally bad weather and gone down. . . . but three was a number that preyed on the mind. It suggested that something more than coincidence was at work. Even to *me,* it suggested that more than coincidence was at work.

Thirty-seven years had passed since a man named Verheyden had taken a ship named *Floreat* out of Lambda's main harbor and headed west across the ocean. That span of time—a generation and a half—was testimony to just how seriously the colony took its loss. A colony that has to fight hard against starvation through every winter can't afford to put men and money into projects which come to less than nothing, no matter what kind of principle is at stake. If Nieland didn't return, it would be thirty-seven years more before another man like him managed to win approval for a similar expedition.

"What of your experiments?" Nieland asked me. "Have you found anything of interest?"

"I've only a light microscope," I told him. "All I'm able to do is look at the plankton samples and the weed. I can't possibly find anything that the survey team didn't . . . and there's hardly likely to have been any significant change in the marine population here in two hundred years. Really, this fetish for taking samples is a little absurd. But it's routine—there's a formularized pantomime we have to go through on every world, so that we can present the UN with a computer printout that weighs three tons, and thus justify our work here. There are always people who will ask what we've done to justify the colossal expense of sending us here. It's not enough that we can say that we helped one or two colonies out of grave difficulties, showed them the way to success. You can't measure things like that. The people who sent us need something with *bulk,* something they can literally *weigh,* and say, "*This* is a contribution to human knowledge and the welfare of our colonies on other worlds. It's the political mind, you know . . . can't deal with abstracts at all."

He looked at me as if he thought I was sending him up. Essentially, he was a politician himself.

Ling smiled. Briefly.

"It's not what we achieve that counts back home," said Mariel, in a gentler tone. "It's what we can be *seen* to have achieved. The UN can't see the worlds themselves. All they can see is our reports, our measurements, our records. They have to be complete. Every moment of our time has to be accounted for, because every moment is costing the taxpayers of Earth real money."

Nieland understood. He understood perfectly. Because his problem was ours, in miniature. His project, like ours, had been funded grudgingly. Like ours, it was a project whose purpose was hard to assess in terms of money. Like us, he had to have something to show for it at the end. He had to make some kind of profit. Unlike us, he couldn't do it by sheer weight of paperwork and the ritualistic pretense that facts and figures were additions to the sum of human understanding. He needed something more obvious than that.

In the long run, so would we. If the space program were to be revived we'd have to come up with some very good reasons for its revival. We had set out not knowing quite what we might find to serve our purpose, but determined to find something. (I, at least, was determined. I sometimes had my doubts about my companions.) Nieland was in very much the same sort of position. He felt that it was wrong that the colony should adopt a policy of determined insularity in search of solutions to its problems. He felt, without perhaps having any real reason for his feeling, that the answer might lie beyond the horizon, across the ocean. He felt that it was *necessary* that the colony should have *something* beyond its horizons, lest those horizons shrink and the colony should die without ever having investigated the possibilities open to it. Such a feeling can be a hard thing to justify, in economic terms.

I think that Nieland looked to me for moral support. And he also hoped that I might find whatever it was that he was looking for. It was rather touching, in a way. Except that I didn't feel any more capable than he did, save in the more optimistic flights of my wildest imagination.

"Your men will be pleased," said Ling to Ogburn. "They will be very glad to sight land."

Ogburn was already rising from his chair, pouring the last of his coffee-substitute down his throat.

"Haven't yet," he said, gruffly, as he moved toward the door. "An' the land may be wo'se than the sea."

He left, slamming the door behind him.

11

"Cheerful soul," I commented. It was not the first time I'd passed the comment. It was getting to be a cliché.

"I wouldn't bank on our landfall coming as any relief," said Mariel to Nieland. "The only thing that would make them happy would be to turn tail and run with the wind behind us. They're a long way from home now, and the money you paid out to them when they signed on is a long way away, along with all the things it can buy. The bonus they get on completing the trip doesn't look a tenth as attractive now as it did then. I think there'll be trouble."

"I think we can trust Ogburn," said Ling.

"He's a strong man," said Nieland. "He'll keep them in line."

Mariel bowed her head, deferring to their statements out of diplomacy. The question that was in her head, and mine, was: Who's going to keep *him* in line? But we left it unvoiced, and let silence descend.

Outside, we could hear the tiny sound of little wavelets lapping against the timbers.

For the millionth time, I wished I'd never set out on this lousy trip. I felt very sorry for Mariel, who had much the same feeling, but also the desperate knowledge that this was the only hope of her reaching the aliens . . . her only hope of making the contact which was her reason for being here.

2

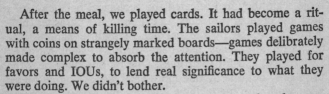

After the meal, we played cards. It had become a ritual, a means of killing time. The sailors played games with coins on strangely marked boards—games deliberately made complex to absorb the attention. They played for favors and IOUs, to lend real significance to what they were doing. We didn't bother.

"At least we'll have some real work to do when we land," said Nieland. "They'll have no time for grumbling when we've land to clear and a base to build. And there'll be fresh food. Things will get better." He was still trying to convince himself.

"You can't blame them too much," said Ling. "We're a long way from home. So far that some of the hardness has been knocked out of them—or perhaps I should say drained. They're afraid, and they don't like being afraid. It's not something that usually afflicts them."

By the standards that Mariel and I applied the ocean wasn't so vast. We'd seen half a dozen worlds now (Earth included) and we measured *our* journeys in light-years. But for these men distance was only meaningful in terms of how far a man could walk, or ride, or sail. Delta was more remote from Lambda than the Earth was, in some ways. *Terra incognita.* They had memories of Earth—not actual ones but histories handed down by word of mouth. Delta was known to them only through dead, technical survey reports.

The colonists had never come to terms with Attica. Not even with the region of Lambda where they had established themselves. They had never managed to get ahead of the game. Things had gone wrong from the beginning—little things, but too many to cope with easily. Like the colonies Kilner had visited, this colony had had a hard time. The local life-system had reacted against the invasion in a thousand subtle ways. After the first few years of establishing their crops and building their homes and planning all the great things that they were going to do the colonists had found a tide slowly turning against them. The crops from Earth had begun to yield less and less as time went by. They had developed allergy problems.

When they had tried to cultivate local produce on a large scale they had affected the ecological balance of the area and created problems. Local pests and parasites, normally controlled by the balance of nature, had become uncontrollable. They had been forced to fight for their sustenance, and for their lives. One by one, they beat the problems, but one by one more emerged. A colony on an alien world, no matter how effective the survey has been, has a great deal to learn, and the processes of learning can be expensive.

Lambda's colony had never managed to get into the positive feedback loop in which their endeavors would have made subsequent endeavors much easier. All their efforts had been sidetracked into the simple battle for survival. They had faced no major crises, but one long enduring series of sub-crises. They had not managed to start their industrial revolution, despite knowing how. They knew where to find the iron ore, the coal, the oil . . . but they just could not free the manpower to begin the necessary flow of supplies.

Knowing how had, in a way, made it worse. It had made them frustrated, had given them a bitter sense of failure.

The visit of the *Daedalus* would almost certainly turn the battle their way. Our laboratory could put right their food-supply problems without too much difficulty. We could engineer their crops to suit the changed circumstances, and help to eliminate the pests. At the very least we could win them another decade's breathing space. On top of what they already had, that should be enough. The feedback process would begin.

But our arrival hadn't made them any happier. In a way, it had reminded them of their failure. They had not made it on their own. Now they needed help. They

14

resented our coming. They resented the necessity of what we had come to do. I couldn't blame them for that.

I'd left Conrad and Linda to take care of the routine work in the colony, largely because I felt that it was my turn to join Mariel as part of the contact team. I'd felt guilty at the time, but now I was regretting my determination. I felt I'd missed out on Wildeblood, remaining in the colony while Conrad and Linda went with Mariel, but by now I was quite prepared to miss out again, if only I could be sure that this particular expedition would some day sail safely home. Curiously, I would have felt a lot safer had there been someone else along. The responsibility of being Mariel's sole companion and guardian weighed a little heavy upon me. But there had been no way that we could spare another biologist, and Karen had been required because there was a good deal of work to be done on the ship's equipment and stores. We hadn't had much of a chance to effect repairs on Arcadia; we had to do work now if we were going to complete our mission by going on to a sixth world.

"The trouble is," I mused, aloud—feeling obliged to make some contribution to the anxious conversation—"that they really are going to find Delta alien. The two continents were never connected at any time during the entire geological history of this planet. Such continental drift as there has been has simply been a partial fragmentation of the initial land masses. The living things on the two continents have to go right back to the initial invasion from the sea to find a common ancestry—and even there the characteristic marine fauna of *this* continental shelf is very different from that of Lambda's except at the microscopic level.

"Delta is much more heavily forested than Lambda over the entire southern bulge, except for a grassland plain in the middle and some mountainous regions. Only in the north, where it begins to thin out into the curlicue do you have conditions similar to those in the colony. The colony has a complex weather pattern because of the relative nearness of the three seas, but Delta doesn't. Its rainfall is much more seasonal. That's why the colony was planted on Lambda, of course—but it also means that

Delta has evolved a life-system very different from what you're used to. Most significantly, there are the aliens. But it's not just them. The birds you saw resting in the rigging are unfamiliar species—and every other species of bird, animal or reptile that we see will be unfamiliar, too. It isn't the kind of terrain your men are used to. They're not going to be able to feel at home there."

I could have added more. I could have added that the aliens themselves were likely to prove fearsome. They would be about a head taller than Ogburn, who was a big man by colony standards—even the females would be his size—and their faces would have what seemed to a human to be an inherent ferocity—a nose like a cat's, with the same split upper lip and front teeth built for rending as much as for slicing. Their ears would be perched high at the sides of their heads, tufted like those of a lynx. Their bodies would be covered with a light but usually highly colored fur, dappled yellow and brown. They would be bipedal, but would be bound to give the impression of a gorilla rather than a man.

"We have to think of something to maintain our equilibrium," said Nieland. "I'd offer them more money, but it isn't mine to offer, and we're a long way from the places they can spend it. I almost wish that I could promise them loot of some kind . . . an El Dorado lost in the forests. Something that would make their minds come alive."

"That's a dangerous policy," I said.

"And they wouldn't believe me anyhow," he added.

I glanced at Mariel, knowing that she wasn't going to like my next suggestion, but seeing no alternative.

"We've only one reasonable incentive to offer them," I said. "And that's to offer to shorten our stay. Say that if they get the base established quickly, and can make contact with the aliens without much trouble, then we'll cut our stay by half. If they know that the faster we get things done the faster we can go home, they'll work."

"It won't leave us enough time," said Mariel. "I have to have time."

"These men don't have our sense of mission," I told her gently. "They're not stupid men, or even particularly

16

unreasonable men . . . but you know their priorities and understand their anxieties better than anyone. You know that our aims mean nothing to them. If we try to force them to do everything our way they're just going to get angrier. They already think we're insane."

"You may say they're not stupid," she said, "but they have closed minds. They're not willing to listen to argument. That's not reasonable."

"All the more reason for compromise," I said. "If we can't make them see our way of thinking . . . then we have to concede ground to theirs."

"It seems a pity," said Ling.

"But there'll be another day," said Nieland. "Once we've been here and returned home, the dam is broached. We'll have proved it can be done. That's the main thing. We can always come back."

"*You* can," said Mariel.

"Our first priority is to help the colony," I reminded her. "The contact mission is secondary. You know that I think it's important—hell, you know that I feel almost as strongly as you do. But it won't be the end of everything if you can't follow through as you'd like to. You've already achieved a great deal on Wildeblood. You don't have to prove yourself all over again."

"You don't understand," she said. The way she said it made me feel that I didn't.

"Nevertheless," I said, "that's how we're going to do it. We establish the base. We try to make contact. If they're ready to come and talk to us, okay. But if they're not interested we're not chasing them . . . and if they show any sign of hostility we get out. Fast."

"That doesn't give me a *chance* to get over any barriers," she complained. "And these people *need* that chance. Who else is going to get over any difficulties the way I could? Is there anyone in the colony with the gift of tongues? If the other expeditions really *were* destroyed by the aliens then my talent may be the only hope we have of finding out why and making sure that it doesn't happen again. The colony can't isolate itself forever . . . someday, now or in a thousand years, it's going to have to contact the aliens."

"Miss Valory," said Nieland, gently. "We have other things to think of. We will establish contact with the natives one day. It is not necessary that it should be done now. Your talent might help. I believe that it would. But this may not be the time. We have to go at our own pace."

I could see that she was fighting tears of disappointment. But she seemed to be winning. The voyage hadn't been easy on her—the crew weren't the best of traveling companions. There were other women on board, but that didn't make her invisible. There are times when it must be pretty near hell to be able to read the thoughts of the people looking at you . . . especially if you're an adolescent girl.

When we'd finished playing the hand we put away the cards. We had killed the game. I took Mariel back to her cabin, and left Ling to talk it over with Nieland. Somehow they'd work out a convenient formula for haggling with the crew.

3

—●—

"It's a bad break," I said, settling down on the floor. The cabins weren't exactly *de luxe*. I had a table and a little leg room. Mariel had only the bunk.

She lay down on the bed and stared up at the ceiling. The lamp was attached to the wall above the pillow, and it cast a shadow across her face when she put up a hand to shield her eyes from its direct glare. I couldn't see her expression.

"It's okay," she said. "I know how things are. They're an ugly lot and they're in a bad mood. But it just seems so ridiculous that we can be beaten by such a stupid thing. After the Salamen, I was *sure* I could talk to these people, *sure* I could get to know them. I was convinced that I could learn more about them in six weeks than an army of exobiologists in six years. I *am* convinced . . . but to come so close and not get the chance. . . ."

"I'm sorry," I said.

"It's not your fault. I'm as worried as you are. They're unpredictable because they're so tense."

"Are they giving you any trouble?" I asked awkwardly.

The question embarrassed her as much as it did me. "No," she said. "They just look. If I couldn't get used to that . . . where would I be? Even back on Earth, when I was fourteen. . . ."

Now she was eighteen. She'd grown into her rather gangly frame. She looked a lot less awkward. She was plain, but she wasn't unattractive.

"It's not your last chance," I said quietly. "The next world has alien indigenes, too. And after that . . . if all goes well. . . ."

"If," she said. She said it very flatly, very bitterly.

"You're afraid, aren't you?" I said. "Afraid of your talent . . . burning out."

She turned on her side to look at me, as if astonished

by my perception. She was used to knowing what other people thought. She wasn't used to them knowing what *she* was thinking.

"How. . . ?" she began.

She stopped, because she could see what I was thinking. Put into words, it was something like: *I'm not a fool. Even I'm not totally insensitive.*

"They do, you know," she murmured. "They always do."

"Maybe people just learn to hide them," I said.

"And maybe they learn to destroy them," she said, softly. "To save themselves.

"Is that what you want to do?"

"No. It's the last thing in the world I'd like to do. I don't believe it. I believe that talents have to die, because if they don't . . ."

". . . people go crazy," I finished for her. "Not necessarily. Nobody knows."

"*I* know," she said, in a fierce whisper. "When you're a child, it doesn't matter. A child is outside the adult social world . . . self-involved, self-possessed. All children are mad, by adult criteria. But as they grow up, we expect them to become sane. How can you take your place in the adult world when you can read minds? When so much depends on rules and conventions and ethics and self-concealment . . . how can there be any place in a world like that for something like me?"

"We've adjusted," I said. "Aboard the ship. Even me. It's four and a half years now. Maybe I took a long time. But I've adjusted now. We all have."

"The ship's a microcosm," she said. "Not a world. It's just six people, forced to live so close to one another that there can't be any such thing as privacy. We all know one another's souls inside out. What does a little thought-reading matter? But in the real world . . . in the complex world of millions of people, where no one knows anyone except perhaps inside marriage, and maybe not then . . . I'm outside. I'm an offense against life itself. As a child, I was a freak . . . but as a *person,* passing myself off as a person. . . ."

"Stop it," I said.

20

She curled up a little, as though her body were instinctively seeking a foetal position which it could no longer quite accomplish. Her eyes were still on my face.

"Do you know what I believe?" she said, in a strange tone that didn't quite belong to her voice. "I believe that talents vanish like magic with virginity. The moment I initiate myself into the human race, it'll be gone just like *that*!"

I looked away. "You can't believe everything," I said, trying to find a way to veer away from the subject. "Not all at once."

"Yes I do," she answered. "All the conflicting theories—all the cute psychological analyses. I believe them all. I believe that I'll have to lose my talent to stay sane. I believe that it will vainsh away like a childhood neurosis once my formal initiation into the wonders of sex is over. I believe it all. And now you see why I can't be sure that there'll be another chance. Ever."

"If it does fade away," I said, again awkwardly, "it won't be the end of the world."

"It won't be the beginning," she said, bitterly.

"Even if there was to be no other opportunity," I said—slowly, because I was treading dangerous ground—"you wouldn't have failed. What you did on Wildeblood . . . you'll always have that. And that was important. That was the *first*. No one can ever take that away from you. You made contact—*real contact*—with an alien species. You got inside their heads, into their way of thinking. No one can deny you that one success. Maybe you'll get a chance to repeat it, maybe you won't. The situation here doesn't look too good. But you mustn't get into this state of bitter desperation. You *mustn't*."

I had built up pace and intensity while I spoke. I watched her relax slightly. Her eyes, with the pupils gaping in the dim light, were fixed upon my face as she looked right into my mind. She could probably have offered a clearer description of what was there than I could.

"Thanks, Alex," she murmured.

"For what?" I asked, uneasily.

"For caring."

There were little tears in the corners of her eyes.

21

I wished that Karen was with us. Or Linda. They, I felt sure, could have done a much better job of caring. It wasn't really my line. It didn't involve examination, analysis and taking census. They were my fortés. Empathy I was always short of.

"Just fight it," I said, feeling that something that sounded like advice was called for. "You have the power. Power to look inside people's heads—and the power to support the power. It's a matter of keeping it all straight. Don't let it slip. Don't let *anything* hurt you. I'll do everything I can to get you another chance. Everything. But if it doesn't work out . . . don't hurt yourself."

She shut her eyes. It was a kind of signal. She was letting me alone . . . taking the pressure off. It was a chance to think something that she wouldn't see, but I knew full well how meaningless that chance really was.

Among the Salamen, I remembered, she'd been *happy*. Maybe the first and only time she ever *had* been happy. How comforting to be among aliens, when you can be free from the double vision that afflicts you among your own kind. She expected a lot from the aliens of Delta. Maybe far too much. Even after one success, there was no way to be sure that they wouldn't have a bad effect on her . . . like the people of Dendra. The Salamen had been amphibians—remote from humanity. Maybe just remote enough.

I stood up, and touched her lightly on the shoulder.

"All right?" I asked.

"Sure," she replied.

I closed the door quietly behind me, and went to my own cabin, next door. I had to pick my way very carefully to the bed—the floor was very cluttered. Once there, I sat down. Almost automatically, I took up a sample of seawater from the table and dipped in a pipette, to take droplets for a series of slides. It wasn't really work—just something to settle my mind, and to make it change gear.

It was very late when I finally went to sleep.

4

If the findings of the first *Daedalus* mission were lumped in with our findings so far, then the Attica colony could be identified as "normal." The others we had visited were, in one way or another, "aberrant"—affected by unique factors. The pattern of slow and steady decline—or, at least, failure to progress—which we found here was a repeat of something Kilner had found no less than four times. Forewarned of the probability, we had been charged with the task of finding out why. We knew that it wouldn't be a simple answer.

Before we had set sail, Nathan had warned me not to underestimate the importance of Attica in our series of scheduled stops. If we were to present a good case for the resumption of the space program, then we would have to take into account all six of the worlds at which we were supposed to call. Some of the situations we'd found looked very bad, some looked passably good. But each of the first four, he reminded me, was a unique case. Each of them might be set aside as atypical if the argument got very tight. But not Attica. Attica was typical. There were a lot of colonies like this one. If the debate were to come anywhere near deadlock—if the vote ran close—then our performance on Attica might well be the deciding factor. Here, our findings could be generalized.

Our joint brief was to discover whether the failure of such colonies as this one was accountable to biological or sociological reasons. And whichever it was, we were supposed to come up with some plan of action which might avert future difficulties of the same kind.

It was easy enough to obtain a historical map of the failure. The first few good years had brought in a good supply of food—enough to support more than half the colony in work that was not primarily productive—like building houses and locating resources: coal, iron, copper,

23

oil, salt, *etc., etc.* All these things were accessible, and the colonists even knew where to look, thanks to the survey reports. But resources can't be exploited with bare hands. To secure each supply the others were necessary. To get at the coal you have to have the iron, and to work the iron ore you have to have the coal. You have to work your way into the feedback loop, a little at a time. To begin with, everything is difficult—even making soap and brick and glass and cloth. It all has to be done the hard way. It continues to be difficult for many years, but with every small triumph it gets a little easier, and then easier, and then easier still . . . and then progress lifts off along an exponential curve.

In theory.

It had happened that way on Floria. It was happening on Wildeblood. But in both cases the process had received some kind of boost—unforeseen and with hidden snags. So far we had not found a single case where the takeoff had happened without some kind of extra assistance.

The basic needs of a colony are simple: machines and power. Iron and fuel. With these, you can *make* everything else you need. But to begin with you have just one kind of machine—body machines, human and animal. Muscle power is the only significant energy reserve you can exploit, with what aid you can co-opt from wind, water and burning wood. The extent to which muscle power can be devoted to the difficult business of making the first machines and finding the first supplies of fuel is controlled by a simple equation: the amount of manpower required to produce enough food to maintain each man. If every man has to work full-time just to supply his own needs there can never be progress. If one man's efforts can supply the food needed by a thousand, it doesn't take long to reach takeoff.

In the beginning, the colony's food-making was efficient. Efficient enough. But after ten years it began to decline, and it continued to decline, as the local life-system reacted against the invasion. At a time when more and more manpower should have been liberated year by year in the cause of progress, year by year more and more manpower had to be returned to the farms and the fields, to clear and plant new land because the land already cleared was failing in its yield, to fight a long, long battle on the land already under cultivation. Insecticides became more important than iron; the selection of crops to find strains which could cope with the responses of the local life-system became more important than coal. The fight for survival from one year to the next, in all it entailed, became the sole aim. The fight for progress was stillborn.

Those were the ecological reasons for failure.

But ecological crises are reflected in social priorities. In the beginning, the colony had an efficient governing body, capable of co-ordinating the efforts of the whole colony. They could ask for men to work for the benefit of the whole and be answered. But as circumstances changed, that became more and more difficult. As it became more difficult for men to support themselves it became more difficult to ask them to work for the whole rather than for themselves. As the fight for survival became more basic the holistic qualities of the colony were steadily eroded. Priorities retreated, as men stopped working for the whole in favor of working directly for themselves or for the local groups where mutual cooperation in working the same land was necessary. As there were fewer men to spare the category of administrators had to shrink. The government itself had to fragment, especially as the colony had to expand in all directions to continually bring new land under cultivation. The colony dispersed and broke up, with each group becoming insular, trading with others but united only in the medium of exchange which they used.

Put simply, the government lost control. They could no longer plan the long-term development of the colony. They could no longer command such spare manpower as there was, because it owed its first loyalty to the local community. The civil service, such as it had ever been, shrank in numbers and became all but impotent. Taxes were collected, and there was always money to hire men for particular projects, but there were few men to be hired. The administrators of the colony had to be very selective indeed in deciding what should be done and when—what kind of "collective endeavors" the colony as a whole (a ghost of a whole) could embark upon.

That was why there had been only four attempts in more than a hundred years to build ocean-going ships. That was why the *New Hope* was a wooden ship entirely dependent upon the wind. The colony on Lambda had the knowledge and—theoretically—the technology to build a ship of steel, powered by steam, but it would have been too expensive to do so. Too expensive since materials were in extremely short supply because of the extremely short supply of manpower. Wood was cheap, and so was the wind. The crew wasn't . . . and neither had been the men who labored to build the ship.

Now, because of its disintegration, it would take a long, long time to bring the colony together again. With the *Daedalus* and its laboratory at their disposal, the government of the colony could turn the tide of the agricultural problems. We could fight the pests, remodel the crops, bring the land back to life. But we couldn't remake the way of thinking that had come into the colony. We couldn't restore the sense of collective identity. We couldn't break down the insularity which had developed in the scattered elements of the colony, or the resentment they had developed with regard to taxation and the "parasitic" civil service which existed on those taxes. When the corner was turned, and things began to get better, it seemed likely that each local community would go its own way, that there would be mistrust and hostility and conflict between them. Progress would take care of itself—manpower not released to the central government would be released into entrepreneurial activities. All that would be lost would be what the colony had started out with: unity and purpose.

And that would be bad—or, to take the cynical view, it would *appear to the UN* to be bad. Because the whole point of sending colonies out from Earth was to get away from mistrust, hostility and conflict. There was a very considerable body of opinion on Earth which said that man had no right to pollute the galaxy until he had solved his problems on Earth. If we brought back evidence that the colonies were inescapably reproducing all those features which on Earth were considered evils, then a very large brick would be knocked out of the edifice of argument by which we might seek to resume the colony project.

I was already certain in my own mind that the ecological problems here could be solved. I was prepared to predict that another *Daedalus* in a hundred years' time would find the colony a lot better off in terms of its technological development and its agricultural performance. I had felt guilty about leaving so much of the work to Conrad and Linda, but I wouldn't have done so if I hadn't been absolutely sure that there were no major difficulties.

But Nathan Parrick wasn't in the least convinced that the social situation was—or could be made—satisfactory. Satisfactory, that is, to the UN.

"It's important that this trip should succeed," he had said, on the night before the *New Hope* set sail. "Important to the colony, but maybe even more important to us. It will allow us to show in our reports—and to argue when the time comes—that the colony is still capable of acting as a whole, that even in the face of adversity it is trying to widen its horizons. Crossing oceans in wooden ships is the kind of gesture that people appreciate—symbolic of triumph over circumstance. This trip has a heroic dimension that the government—and we—will be able to exploit. If it succeeds. The failure of the earlier trips will add extra mystique to its triumph."

He always talked like that. The symptoms of a perverted sense of values. But I knew enough to realize that what he said was probably true enough, however perverted. To him, almost everything we encountered was advertising copy. Pro or anti. The voyage of the *New Hope* was not only no exception, it was an example *par excellence*. It was romantic, nostalgic, impressive.

"What would you like us to find at the other end?" I had asked, dryly.

"The aliens, of course," he said. "A new continent is fair to middling. Echoes of Columbus . . . it has its mythical resonances. But the aliens add something else. They represent the face of the unknown. If anything can jerk this colony out of its introverted priorities it's contact with aliens. There's nothing else that will restore to them any real sense of collective identity or solidarity."

27

"Perhaps you'd like me to arrange a war?" I asked. "An alien invasion of Lambda. There's nothing like a common enemy to unite people, so the cliché says. A good war fires national enthusiasm like nothing else."

It's a stupid cliché," observed Nathan. "The so-called national spirit that emerges at the time of war is itself nothing more than a propaganda device. It isn't real. It's an illusion conjured up by the government in the hope of forcing national spirit upon the people. The last thing we need is war. War with the aliens is exactly what the let's-not-export-our-sins-to-the-galaxy brigade need to sink the colony project forever. And at a more mundane level, if the aliens *did* invade Lambda—assuming, that is, that the aliens have any political entity capable of managing a war—they'd almost certainly conquer it with no trouble."

"There is that," I agreed, sarcastically.

"What *we* need," said Nathan, "and what the colony needs, of course, is some kind of symbol of peaceful cooperation. Hands across the sea. A meeting of minds. That sort of thing."

"You want me to bring back a peace treaty and make political speeches? Maybe a pipe of peace? Gifts of elephants and exotic silks?"

"If you could manage it," he said, with equanimity, "yes."

With such ideas in mind—even as kitschy metaphors—we had sailed with optimism in our hearts. That was the way the voyage had been set up—a *gran geste,* a publicity stunt.

Now, a couple of days from shore, I didn't feel nearly so good. In fact, I didn't feel good at all. Neither did Nathan. I reported in every morning by radio, and explained the situation. There was never much news beyond the fact that things were getting steadily and irrevocably worse. Nathan had run out of encouraging suggestions weeks before. If he'd been that way inclined he'd be praying for miracles by now.

I told him what we'd decided about cutting our trip short.

"It means no hands across the sea," I told him. "No

peace treaties. If we even see the aliens it'll be a quick hello/good-bye."

"It's okay," he said. "Salvage what you can. Better a hint of success than a total failure. Come back with what you can, but at all costs come back."

"They made a good story out of *Mutiny on the Bounty*," I commented.

"Sure," he said. "But *Mutiny on the Santa Maria* would be a pretty sick story compared with *Columbus Discovers America*. Be careful."

"If only," I said, as I signed off, "my being careful was all that was required."

5

There was a knock at the door, and it was unceremoniously yanked open. I was glad that it opened outwards— it could have done a lot of damage if it had been hurled into the cluttered space within.

The man who leaned through the doorway, reaching out a big, horny hand, was Ogburn.

"Binoc'lars," he said, with his usual economy.

A funny rejoinder occurred to me, but I didn't use it. I handed him the binoculars instead.

"Why?" I asked.

But he was already gone.

I jumped to the conclusion that we had sighted land, and followed him at a rapid pace. It seemed as if a great weight was about to be lifted from my mind. But when I got on deck, there was nothing in sight but the mottled green sea. Ogburn was balanced on the rail on the starboard side of the ship, with his elbow hooked into the rigging. He wasn't even looking to the west, but to the north.

I shaded my eyes and squinted slightly, following the direction of his gaze. There was, in fact, something on the horizon.

An off-white triangle.

A sail.

Ogburn jumped down, and with an uncharacteristically graceful gesture, handed me the binoculars. I focused them quickly. I saw that the edges of the triangle were curved, and that the sail was vaguely reminiscent of that carried by an arab dhow. I couldn't see the body of the craft beneath it. It was sailing away from us, disappearing beyond the horizon.

"Do we chase?" asked Ogburn.

I considered for a moment. While I was considering, Nieland joined us, having been alerted to the fact that something was up. I handed him the glasses and waited for him to react. It was really his decision.

"We must be near land," he said, when he lowered the binoculars.

"We already know that," I said.

"Keep heading west," he said to Ogburn.

Ogburn looked dubious. He seemed to be about to make some perceptive comment, but then decided against it. It took a few more seconds for me to realize what was wrong.

Nieland realized too. "But they haven't got sailing ships!" he complained. "Only canoes."

So, at least, said the survey report.

"The survey team only surveyed Delta from the air," I reminded him. "They didn't make any contact with the natives. Everything they said about them was based on photographic evidence. And it was two hundred years ago. They could have missed the sailing ships. It's even possible that the sail was invented some time during the last couple of centuries. Times change."

"It was a big boat," put in Ogburn. "Funny sail for a fishing boat."

He didn't sound too rapturous about it.

"How big?" I asked.

"Sixty footer," he replied.

"That's not big," said Nieland. "Not by comparison with the *New Hope*."

There was a certain proprietary pride in this expostulation. But I knew what Ogburn meant. It was big by comparison with a canoe. And the sail design was really quite sophisticated. From the canoe to the dhow in two hundred years? It didn't seem likely. The survey team must have missed the sailing boats. Unless. . . .

"The other expeditions," I mused, speaking aloud. "They never got back. But that's not to say that they never got *here*. . . ."

"We should go after it," said Ogburn.

"It's going away from us," said Nieland. "It's already out of sight. There's no point in chasing it all day. Let's make landfall first and worry about it later."

He was very impatient. To him, the only thing that

31

mattered was getting there. I sympathized—and Ogburn didn't really want to press his case.

Behind us, a couple of the crewmen were muttering. I knew them as Roach and Thayer. They were making unkind and ominous remarks about the sail and about us. Ogburn ignored them. He didn't even tell them to get back to work. Instead, he signaled to the mate—a man named Malpighi—and gave him the binoculars, which he plucked from Nieland's hand without asking.

"Send a man up top," he grunted. "Keep a lookout."

Malpighi selected Thayer. While he was beginning the long climb up the mainmast Roach slouched away. He glanced at me, and said: "Gone to fetch the fleet, I shouldn't wonder. Blow us out of the water. Probably what happened to Verheyden."

It looked like the beginning of a rumor which, if not exactly ugly, could hardly contribute to the morale of the ship's personnel. But there was nothing I could do except give him a dirty look. He scowled back.

I glanced at Ogburn. "If I were a fisherman and I saw something like the *New Hope*," I said, "I'd run for home and tell them I saw one *this big*. And they wouldn't believe me."

He didn't laugh.

I couldn't blame him.

The party broke up. Nieland began setting the position of the sun on his sextant—his regular ritual of position-finding. We were still cutting through the weed without any trouble, and the wind was blowing from the southwest, which was about as favorable as we were likely to get. It was brisk enough to be turned to our advantage. I decided to do some fishing, and went below to get some line and a few hooks. I didn't really care whether I caught anything or not.

The day wore on at its customary turgid pace—it was about two hours longer than an Earthly day, but there were a few less of them in the planetary year, which was only a couple percent longer than standard. By now I was an expert at letting the time pass unheeded, and I managed to occupy myself while retreating into the privacy of my contemplation. I always did fancy myself a spiritual descendent of Newton: "A mind forever voyaging through strange seas of thought—alone."

I thought mainly about the aliens, wondering why a dhow was sailing so far south. The most civilized region of Delta was a long way north of here—we'd deliberately set out to sail across the ocean the shortest way, which brought us to the bulge of the lower part of the small-case *delta*. There was nothing but forest here, and the aliens in the forest—according to the two-hundred-year-old survey reports—were iron age swidden farmers without much iron. Not the type of people who'd suddenly take to the sea.

Did that mean that the aliens had come on a fair bit and were sallying forth on exploratory odysseys? Or did it mean that the colony—unknown to itself—had fathered a little colony here on the alien shore, whose inhabitants were (for reasons best known to themselves) minding their own business instead of letting the prevailing wind carry the good news back home?

I was tempted to toss a coin, but I was never a great believer in oracles.

Three fish and a lot of drifting on strange seas of thought later, my attention was once again snatched back to matters close at hand.

Thayer, from his lonely station aloft, called out in tones as stentorian as they were portentous: "I can see the shore!"

My first thought, idiotically, was one of disappointment. The fool hadn't read his script. Everyone knows you're supposed to shout *"Land ho!"* Then you add something about the port bow.

I wished that I had my binoculars, but I've no head for heights and it didn't seem to be a good idea to go fetch them. I waited for Ogburn to wave Thayer down and commandeer them himself, and then I joined him on the roof of the wheelhouse, from which we both craned our necks to get a glimpse of the promised land.

For a while, I thought that Thayer's optimism had over-reached itself. Because of the weed the surface of the sea was mostly green with lacunae of gray and brown—from above it might have looked much like marshy

33

land—and it wasn't easy to spot a change of color or texture in the line of the horizon. But it was there all right—eventually I could pick out the silvery foam of waves breaking on rocks, and then the lighter green of foliage extending beyond.

Nieland came up on deck, and promptly got out his sextant. I was glad to be able to laugh. Even Ogburn came to life a little more than usual as he began handing out orders in some profusion. Nieland proved that he wasn't just wasting his time by demonstrating that we were very close to the mouth of a major river, which ought to prove navigable for quite some distance as it wound inland through the forest. Ogburn agreed to make for the river, and we found our way into its estuary late that afternoon. We proceeded slowly, with a man taking soundings every yard of the way, but the bottom was a long way down and the river was wide.

There were mudbanks on the north bank, caused not by tidal effects (Attica's moon was only a fifth the size of Earth's) but by the fact that the river's dimensions varied according to season. The rainy season was well behind us for this year, and the river had shrunk somewhat. We didn't go far upriver—hardly a mile—before we anchored. We lowered the larger of the ship's boats, and held an informal debate as to who would join the party which—at the cost of muddy boots—would be the first human beings (so far as we knew) to set foot on the new continent. There were ten of us in all—the four passengers, Malpighi and five of the crew. We let Nieland step out first. After all, it was his ship.

The day was warm, but hardly tropical. Nevertheless, the forest beyond the mudbar did have a suggestion of jungle about it. It was extremely wet, because the ground had a tendency to bogginess, and the branches of the trees were festooned with creepers. There was a preponderance of long, spatulate leaves and languorous drapes. The tree trunks were gnarled—quite a lot were hairy or scaled like fircones. There was a smell of *staleness*. There were a great many small birds moving along the branches and I saw several green snakes coiling round the stems of the creepers. Midges clustered in vaporous clouds around the shallow pools of brackish water, and the mud seemed to be alive—though much of the movement was caused by tiny bubbles of marsh gas rising to the surface rather than by the small invertebrates and amphibians which inhabited it.

I shook the branches of a particularly wizened tree, and inspected the shower of insects that inevitably resulted with some enthusiasm. Two of the crewmen, standing nearby, left me in no doubt as to their opinion of this eccentric behavior.

I found a lizard with spadelike suckered feet clinging to the bark of a tree pretending to be an excrescence of its trunk, and plucked it off. It wriggled furiously, and let its long black tongue loll out of its mouth. It was toothless, but the upper palate was ridged with rough bone contours that would be quite adequate for crushing the insects on which it fed. I let it go.

There was a constant chatter which—though most of it was made by the birds and other flying creatures—could by no means be described as "song." It was all clicks and rattles, clucks and croaks, with only the occasional half-strangled whistle.

The distribution of the trees was highly irregular—they tended to grow in clumps and thickets, with clearings between where the space might be enjoyed either by waist-high bushes and cane-breaks or by moist sand which looked rather ominous. The crew needed no warnings about not wandering too freely—they showed little inclination to move more than a few yards away from the firm outer rim of the mudbar. There were occasional trees that grew very much taller than the rest, spreading their crowns magnificently and creating oases of shade where grew plants of different character—fleshy things and lichenous crusts.

There was no immediately obvious sign of human habitation.

I took Nieland aside. "We'll have to go some way upriver before we can select a campsite. I don't think there's much point in pressing on tonight with the *New Hope*. Let's fill up the water tanks from the river—I'll check it for potability and we can sterilize if necessary. The crew can get their washing done—and so can the rest of us. If the men want to come ashore here they can, but tell them to stay close by and to move about in pairs. It's not a particularly inviting prospect, so there shouldn't be much dissent. It's time for relaxation. Ask Ogburn if you and I can take the small rowboat upriver—tell him we'll spy out the land and look for a campsite. I just want a look around. I don't expect to see any natives, but if we do we'll stay clear. Mariel will want to come too."

Nieland went off to discuss the matter with Ogburn. There would be no difficulty—it was all common sense.

Mariel turned up beside me. The expression on her face was one of mild distaste.

"Not very nice," she commented. "It's not all like this, is it?"

I shook my head. "Upriver it'll be a lot cleaner. Much of this place gets flooded in the rainy season. A lot of organic detritus gets brought down in the floods and deposited here, trapped by the nets of creepers. That's why there's so much life here . . . not to mention the faint odor of decay."

"A good thing the flies don't fancy human flesh," she commented, looking at the clouds of minute insects.

"There's nothing here will hurt us," I said. "Except poisonous snakes and maybe one or two thorny things. But everyone has the sense to steer clear of things with fangs and stings. The water's okay for bathing."

Nieland returned, and said: "We can take the boat. He's even thrown in Roach to row it."

I had slightly mixed feelings about the latter bit of news, but on balance I decided that it was a good idea. I'm not a great rower, and we would be going against the current. Roach was a solid individual, with arms like a gorilla's.

We set off without any further delay—I was glad to see the back of the ship, and I've no doubt the crew was glad to see the back of us. Of the four of us, Ling was easily the most popular—they wouldn't mind his still being around.

Nieland sat in the prow of the boat, facing front. Roach was behind him, facing Mariel and myself. We both concentrated hard on the banks to either side. At first the south bank was hardly visible, but it soon drew in. It was a steeper shore than the north bank, with rough rocky faces ascending quite sheerly along most of its length. Obviously the south land didn't get flooded even at the height of the wet season. The land to the north remained flatter and decorated by swamp vegetation, though this gradually gave way to a steeper aspect with long, slanting faces of smooth rock interrupted by cracks and crannies where tangled grasses grew. The river flowed slow and deep and had obviously worn out a deep channel over many centuries.

Mariel began to trail her hand in the water—the shore on her side was so much farther away than the shore on mine that there was very little to be seen there.

"Don't," I said.

"Why not?"

"There's usually things in rivers that'll have it off," I said. I pointed to some long, gray shapes sunbathing on the shallow slopes of rock on the north bank.

"Crocodiles?" she asked.

"Something like that," I told her. "Mammals, actually—scavengers and fish-eaters rather than predators, but if they see something pale trailing in the water as if it's dead. . . ."

"I get the message," she said, drying her hand on her sleeve.

"There are predatory reptiles in the sea off the coast here," I said. "More like plesiosaurs—on a small scale—than they are like crocodiles. They may come upriver, too—at least this far."

"I can see why they put the colony on Lambda," said Nieland.

I saw Roach looking suspiciously at the water.

"They won't bother us," I said. "As long as we're careful."

"You said it was safe to bathe," Mariel reminded me.

"The things like plesiosaurs have small heads," I reassured her. "They mostly live on frogs and the like. Nothing round here would size up a human as natural prey. An odd hand trailing in the water is a different matter."

37

Nieland coughed and spluttered. He took something out of his mouth and wiped it off his fingers on the edge of the boat. "Swallowed an insect," he explained.

"Why don't they bite?" asked Roach. "The ones back home do."

"So will these if they get a chance to get used to having humans around," I said. "Human blood offers them as much nourishment as local produce offers us. But it's strange. It'll take them time to adapt and get into the habit. At the moment we smell all wrong. Enjoy your immunity while it lasts."

It would last a good long while yet, I knew. It took about ten years of constant coexistence before the problems of co-adaptation began to rear their ugly heads. As the colony had already discovered by bitter experience.

On the floor, slanted across beneath the seat, was my rifle. It carried three clips of ammunition, but all three were loaded with anaesthetic darts. I was setting a good example. The ship had its own armory, with maybe a dozen shotguns in it. I was hoping that the weapons would stay aboard the ship, largely because one of the things I most wanted to avoid was for the aliens' first contact with humans to be with a panicky crewman armed with a shotgun. Unfortunately, I suspected that the crew of the *New Hope* wasn't going to trust their safety ashore entirely to one outworlder with a gun that fired little needles.

We eventually stopped, tethering the boat to a tree on a mid-stream island. It was only about thirty meters by ten, but it seemed to be quite impressive largely because it was so tall. Its sides were smooth, steep rock for fifteen feet or so up from the surface of the river, and then it was domed with lichen save for a star-shaped depression in its crown, like the depression in a molar tooth, where a variety of flowering plants grew. It wasn't an easy climb to the top, but we managed it with the aid of a slanting crack that wound along the southern face of the rock, and with the help of a couple of tough climbing plants embedded there. Its shoots would have been strong enough to support even Ogburn.

Once at the top I could sit down on the "summit" and

look out over the gentle waters of the great river. We had come around too many bends for the *New Hope* to be visible, but that didn't bother me in the least. What I wanted to see—or at least try to see—was the forest. From down below, at water level, we had been looking up even to the roots of the trees on the bank.

Even from my vantage point on the great tooth I was hardly in a position to look out upon the great green mansions of the glorious forest, but I could see for a fair distance over the crowns of the nearer trees. What I was looking for was smoke.

I scanned the north bank—the nearer one—without success. Then, a long way to the south I spotted a thin grey smudge extending into the deep blue of the sky. If the day had been cloudy, I probably wouldn't have been able to make it out.

I pointed it out to Mariel.

Kilroy was here, all right.

We contemplated the smoke in silence for a couple of minutes. There wasn't anything to say, really. One thought, though, nagged at my mind unvoiced. Whoever was sitting round that campfire wasn't the kind of person who'd be sailing dhows around way out in the weed-belt. When swidden farmers go fishing they use fishing lines in the river. We hadn't even seen a canoe in coming this far up from the sea.

Roach expressed some doubt as to whether we should be standing on the skyline. I pointed out that we could stand off an army from the top of the rock—even one armed with a pocket battleship. He didn't appreciate my making light of it.

"It's a long way back to the ship," he complained.

"Well," I said, "if the mermaids set an ambush we'll just have to fight our way through."

I regretted it immediately as an unnecessarily exasperating remark, but it was done. I resolved to be more diplomatic in future.

"If there are aliens nearby," said Nieland, more reasonably, "they could have seen the boat from the forest at any time. And the *New Hope* isn't inconspicuous. We're not trying to hide from them."

Roach just grunted. He moved to the edge of the rock and spat into the water far below.

"We'd better get back," I said. "We'll have to bring the ship upriver. It might be a mile or two more before we find somewhere suitable to build a base. There's no point in trying to penetrate to the interior in a rowboat."

Roach seemed glad of the decision.

"We need a good night's sleep," agreed Nieland. "Tomorrow the work starts."

That thought didn't seem to gladden Roach's heart.

"We could find another island," suggested the crewman. "A little bigger. That's to be safe."

I was already beginning to lower myself down the gully, and didn't bother to answer him. Mariel followed.

All the way back to the ship, Roach's eyes were scanning the forest above us, searching the shadows for something to be scared of, feeding his own unformed fears.

I knew that our suspicious forebodings were justified. The crew *wasn't* going to be any happier now we'd reached our destination.

At least, I thought, they won't begrudge putting work into the building of a nice strong stockade.

6

The next day we took the *New Hope* upriver. It proved almost impossible to make much headway against the current, gentle as it was, and in the end we came no farther than the toothlike spur of rock which we had reached the previous evening by rowboat. We selected a spot at which there was a relatively shallow slope to the rock face of the northern bank, and found a natural "stairway" which made it easily negotiable. There was an area of loose stone and scrub at the top of the ridge and perhaps fifty meters or so of bush and grass without any large trees before the forest proper began. It looked as if it would be easy enough to clear with nothing heavier than machetes.

And so work began. The crew made short work of clearing out the bushes and scything down the tall grasses, and we pitched half a dozen tents by midday. In the afternoon the heavier work began as the men set about cutting trees to build a stockade round the camp. Ultimately, so the plan went, we would cut much more wood and build cabins.

The sound of axes and saws made a terrific racket, and if the locals hadn't seen us coming up the river in our tall ship then they would surely have known of our presence by the end of the second day. It could have been worse—we had a case of dynamite in the hold which we would have used in blasting a clearing if it had been necessary. Dynamite—nitroglycerine in a soft silica matrix—had been one of the first technological advances the Lambda colony had made. It's a very easy one. Unfortunately, it's no great shakes as a foundation stone of civilization.

Despite my protests Ogburn had broken out half a dozen of the shotguns from the armory. He insisted on having two men—or women—permanently posted as guards (thus reducing our work force by more than five percent), while the other four guns were placed conveniently ready to hand. The whole operation was being supervised by Nieland and Ling, in collaboration with Ogburn. It was not a happy collaboration.

When things seemed to be going moderately well, and I had managed to transfer most of my own equipment from the cramped cabin aboard ship to the not-quite-so-cramped tent on the ridge, I put it to the joint supervisors that it was time to begin the work of laying in supplies from the forest. They were quick enough to agree, having been living off *Daedalus* MDR rations for some time (a rather unappetizing diet if you aren't used to it). I asked for three crew members, the logic being that we would all have to learn to find food eventually, and that the quicker a couple of the crew were able to take on the work the quicker I could stop being a guide and teacher. After a bit of haggling, I got two: the officially designated cook (one of the females) and Roach. I didn't really consider Roach educable in this respect, but he was sent by Ogburn on the basis of his reputation with a gun. The prospect of fresh meat was something that appealed to Ogburn. Ling came along too.

The survey team had landed on Delta only briefly, and had been rather tentative in their explorations. They had steered clear of the aliens and had done most of the actual surveying from the air. The survey report on the fruits of the forest was therefore a little sparse . . . and because of the long isolation of the two continents and the virtually independent evolutionary histories they had enjoyed it wasn't possible to apply lessons learnt on Lambda in any but the most general way. That meant that we would have to proceed partly by trial and error, though much of the equipment I had managed to bring with me was directed to the purpose of testing for nutritional qualities and poisons. In fact, the one thing we could be virtually certain of before starting out was that any local game which we managed to shoot would be edible.

I took along my own rifle, not because I didn't trust Roach's aim (though I had my suspicions) but because it seemed a more civilized weapon. And if anything dangerous turned up, I didn't want to rely entirely on one man

42

and a rather primitive shotgun. I hoped that we wouldn't run into any aliens until the occasion was more propitious.

We scored trees as we went so that we could be sure of finding our way back.

Fruits and nuts aren't as common in forests as is generally made out . . . especially not forests full of fruit-eating birds. Nor, when you do find them, are they always easy to get at. For the first half hour or so I was taking samples in some profusion, more out of scientific interest than because I thought many of them would offer a supply of useful food, but curiosity for curiosity's sake began to wane after a while, and I began to search more rigorously for hopeful growths. In the meantime, Roach grew steadily more impatient. Maybe he had expected to see small deer or big fat birds lurking around every bush. The pace at which we moved irritated him. He wanted to cover more ground in a hurry, stalking his prey with single-minded intensity. He fancied himself quite a hunter, and he thought that the rest of us were cramping his style.

Eventually, he began drifting apart from us—slightly ahead or to one side. Periodically, Ling, the cook and I would stop for discussions about some particular vegetable, considering its abundance, recognizability and possible usefulness. At other times we would dig up roots in search of tubers or other storage organs. These pauses he saw as his chance to make his kill. I didn't say anything about it. He wouldn't have taken it kindly, and I really couldn't bring myself to care much whether he got lost or not.

It was just his luck—and ours—that while he was wandering off on one of his mini-expeditions *we* found the meat.

We had come to a thicket, and were investigating its berries when we heard mewling inside. Ling parted the bushes and stepped into the thick undergrowth before I could say anything. Then he parted the foliage so that we could see. In a "nest" made from matted grasses there was a group of small mammals. They rather resembled pigs or enlarged baby rats. Their eyes were open and they were mobile, but they didn't attempt to run. They just

43

filled their lungs and yelled as hard as they could. That wasn't very hard, as it happened, but it was a thin, penetrative sound.

"Don't!" I said, as Ling reached down to pick up one of the creatures. I was unslinging my rifle, knowing what was about to happen.

"Back out," I said. I didn't have time to say any more.

She burst from the undergrowth away to our right, already at full speed. She came thundering across the open ground. She was about the size of an Alsatian dog, with a rodent-like head and a body that put me in mind of a tapir, striped in brown and white.

She was head on to me and I hit her between the eyes. If you're firing bullets that's not a bad place to hit, but anaesthetic darts aren't intended to go through skulls. She kept coming, refusing even to flinch.

"Get out of the way!" I yelled.

The cook was free to move, and she did—away to the left. I went right, on the principle that you should keep the adversary confused. But Ling was still in the bushes, and he couldn't move at all.

I fired again, getting her neatly in the flank this time. It would put her out for the count, but another unfortunate thing about darts is that they don't work instantaneously. Ling would have been in trouble if the beast had reached him, but the woman swung at the animal with the satchel in which she'd been putting all our souvenirs. It was fairly heavy now, and it caught the pig-thing on the snout. The pig-thing promptly redirected its attack, veering off to the left. The cook was off-balance and I did the only thing I could think of—though looking back it doesn't strike me as a particularly appropriate reaction. I dropped everything and dived forward to catch its tail in both hands.

That *really* made it mad. Trumpeting its rage it doubled back on itself and came at me. Luckily, having given up all its forward momentum, it didn't hit me very hard. It butted me on the shoulder, but didn't use its teeth. I thumped it on the snout.

The beast seemed to remember then what had brought her in the first place, and became once again a mother rushing to the support of her young. She let go another trumpeting sound—this time rather plaintive—and tried to get back to the nest in the thicket.

It was too late. The drug got to her at last and she fell over, unconscious. I leaned over her prostrate form and plucked the first dart out of her head. She was lying on the other one.

Then Roach appeared, belatedly, brandishing his phallic symbol.

I rubbed my shoulder, which was slightly bruised, and ignored him. He didn't stop until he was right on top of me, and when I looked up (I was still sprawled on the ground) I was surprised to see that he was angry. The fact that he'd missed out had really made the bile rise. Then, as I struggled slowly to my feet, the anger ebbed. He took out a knife from his belt and began looking round.

"What are you looking for?" I asked.

"A pole," he said. "We cut a pole, tie her feet together, sling the . . ."

"I know the theory," I said. "But not this time."

"What?" He was holding the knife as if he couldn't wait to stick it into someone.

"Not this one," I told him. "We'll let her be. She'll wake up."

"You're crazy!" he said.

"It's not sporting," I said, gently. "A mother with babies. We're not desperate. We can shoot something else for dinner."

He opened his mouth to say something, then changed his mind. Instead, he said—in a tone which I presume was meant to be reasonable—"We'll take the lot back. This lot'll feed the whole crew. We haven't caught a smell of anything else."

I didn't want to argue. I knew full well we had no common ground on which to debate the issue.

I just said: "No."

"Wait," said Ling. "Sentiment is all very well. But a good meal for all of us . . . it's the first in a long time. We're entitled."

He was right, in his own way. On Attica, my scruples were meaningless. But I came from Earth, where the

45

work of an ecologist is often one long, long fight to conserve species threatened by a sense of values that has no room for them. My prejudices had been deeply ingrained by the experiences of many individual battles.

I hesitated, trying to weigh it all up in my mind, knowing that by all the rules of diplomacy I ought to set my prejudices aside.

Roach didn't give me a chance to give in gracefully. He simply let the muzzle of his gun swivel to point at the sleeping creature's neck, and pulled the trigger.

The shot echoed in the trees on every side.

"It's dead now," he sneered.

Temper rose in me like a flood, and I felt an uncontrollable urge to smash the butt of my own gun into his face. He watched me, and I knew that he'd have loved the excuse to hit me. We were all set for a brawl I had no chance of winning.

I was saved by a new arrival. It wasn't the U.S. Marines come to save us from ourselves. It was daddy, come to kill the lot of us.

I didn't know whether to think of him as a bull or a boar, but whatever he was he was the size of a small donkey and he was as mad as hell. Unlike his late wife he had some very useful weapons dressing his skull—six, to be precise. They were curved tusks, in two rows along the snout. They looked the sort of tool evolution might devise for the job of disemboweling.

He came across the clearing like a tank. I saw him over Roach's shoulder, dropped to one knee and brought up my gun. I never fired it, because Roach put a boot in my chest and shoved. I never knew whether he had seen the charging boar or not. Maybe he was starting a fight, maybe he was just getting me out of the way so that *this* kill could be his.

Either way, Roach turned and raised his gun. He had one barrel left and he let fly. He was too late. The boar was traveling too fast, and that tusked head, with a vicious sideways twist, ran straight into Roach's groin.

He screamed, and screamed again.

I was flat on my back and the beast could have dealt with me with a single leap and a quick flash of the horns,

46

but Roach's shot had peppered its back and head, and it was in no mood for tactical planning. It cut at Roach again, ripping his belly and pulling out his guts like candy floss as he folded up, *still* screaming.

Ling and the woman were running for the trees. I brought the rifle up and pumped out three darts on automatic fire. I managed to get to my feet, and at last the beast abandoned Roach and came for me. I stabbed out at its head with the butt of my gun, and caught it a solid blow. It reeled, and went to its knees—not because of the power of my blow but because the shot and the darts were taking their toll. I hit it again, the same way. It rolled over.

I sat down, suddenly out of breath.

Ling and the woman came back, slowly. I took Roach's gun out of his dead hand and passed it to the woman.

"All right," I said, ignoring their horror-stricken expressions, "now we have the whole family. A real banquet. So much for sentiment."

I felt myself for injuries. There weren't any. But I was trembling a little.

The four babies were still mewling hopelessly. Instinct told them that it was the right thing to do. So much for instinct.

There was blood everywhere. Animal blood, human blood.

"Go back to the camp," I told them. "Quickly. Get some men out here. We're going to need three poles now."

The woman was crying. She knelt over Roach, and she was crying. That shocked me slightly. She was nearly fifty, with graying hair and a face that was set like granite. I couldn't tell whether it was grief or shock that was bringing the tears. Then she looked at me, and there was hatred in her eyes. I couldn't understand why, for a moment or two. I just couldn't see how it added up in her mind to being all my fault. In my book, it was all down to Roach. But that wasn't the way she saw it. It was Roach who was dead, Roach whom she was crying over. I'd picked the argument. She wasn't concerned with all the might-have-beens and the logic of the situation. She didn't care that Roach had paused to kick me out of the way so that I couldn't shoot the creature. It was all my fault and that was all there was to it.

One day ashore, and one man dead.

I knew full well that a good meal wasn't going to square this up. Things were bad, and getting worse.

7

In the evening, we had our feast. Every mouthful reminded us of Roach. We'd done a pretty fair day's work, but that didn't seem to count for anything now.

I called Nathan afterward, and told him the whole sad story. I must have told it slightly wrong, because even he somehow got the idea it was my fault.

"You'd better pray that nothing else goes wrong," he told me. "You'd better pray that the memory fades fast. If there was one thing you could do to fuck up this jaunt any more than it's fucked up already getting a man killed is it. You're a long way from any help, Alex. Remember that. It's all down to you."

"Thanks," I said. "Thanks a lot."

Only half the crew elected to spend the night on land. The rest returned to their bunks below decks. Ogburn posted three armed guards on four-hour shifts throughout the night. I fully expected that the natives would descend upon us at any moment, firing poison darts out of blowguns and wielding battleaxes. Somehow, though, our luck held out *that* far.

Mariel told me that there was a whisper about a curse. I'd heard plenty of talk about bad luck, and it didn't surprise me to learn that the fantasies were being steadily inflated. Nobody *really* believed in curses, but in a situation like that it isn't belief that mattered—it was the power of the fantasies to mesmerize the imagination . . . and the abundance of the fuel of fear. I worried a lot about the way that superstition was taking hold. Prophecies of doom have a nasty propensity for becoming self-fulfilling.

I am not a man who habitually sleeps with his hand on his gun, but that night the rifle was very close to my sleeping bag.

But the next day dawned without anyone trying to murder anyone else, and work began again at a steady pace that was far from frantic. It was a hot day, and the tree-fellers, in particular, built up quite a sweat. Some of the men went swimming at noon, under the watchful eye of a shotgun guard. Nothing untoward happened—the long gray shapes stayed well away.

The stockade grew, and took on a comforting solidity. The first of the huts was marked out on the ground, and the foundations were laid. Another expedition into the forest passed off without mishap, and I made steady progress checking all the possible food sources. I passed most of them as edible, but thought it diplomatic not to call for volunteers immediately. I used only one test subject—myself. I didn't even ask Mariel, whose stomach was of proven sensitivity.

And then, in the afternoon, lightning struck again.

A big, burly man felled one of the giant trees that grew in relative isolation. It was at the northern end of the area outside the stockade that had been cleared, and would have smashed the stockade if it had fallen the wrong way, but he had done his work well. It fell the right way, with no one underneath it. He walked out along its length to inspect his work with justifiable pride. A snake, upset by the upending of its resting place, struck at him from the foliage.

I was with him inside a minute, but there was no way to identify the snake or the kind of poison it had pumped into him. There were three or four different types of poison used by Attican snakes, and this just had to be one of the fast-acting ones. By the time the symptoms were clear enough to treat, his nervous-system was paralyzed. I managed to keep his heart going for an hour or more, but I hadn't the means to save his life. He died before sunset.

That was two down, and I knew that the apple-barrel was really going sour.

In the evening, another hunting-and-foraging party set out. I stayed at home. Nieland took charge. They took three guns, and they looked ready to shoot anything that moved. I hoped that the natives had the sense to stay away. They didn't look ready to play "Take Me To Your Leader" with any seven-foot catmen.

I dissected the snake that had killed our second casualty, and prepared a specific anti-serum for its poison. You never know when things like that will come in handy, though I was certain in my own mind that the next person to get bitten would make sure it was a different species that got him. Such is life. Mariel did some of the routine food tests for me and offered to keep the score if the test specimens I'd eaten should prove to be debilitating. That's what's known as undiplomatic generosity.

But I didn't get ill.

It was just getting dark when a man stuck his head into the tent and said: "Come quick."

It was Thayer, and he had been doing a lot of running—he was panting hard. I recalled that he had gone out with the foraging party. Mariel had gone back aboard ship—as much to avoid my bitter temper as because there was anything still aboard that needed transporting up to the camp. There seemed to be no time to look for her and tell her where I was going.

"It's Ling," gasped Thayer. "He's hurt."

I grabbed the medical kit and pushed past him, without a word. My jaw was set tight. A chapter of accidents was one thing, but this seemed to be verging on the surreal.

Thayer reached into the tent and fished out my dartgun, and also the lantern I'd just switched on.

"I'll bring this," he said. I didn't bother to argue about it. I waited for him to lead the way. He did so, at a fast trot.

We followed a blazed trail that led off at an angle of about sixty degrees from the ill-fated course I'd followed the previous day. Dusk didn't last long, but the fuel-celled electric lamp was quite bright enough for us to find our way from one score-mark to the next. We didn't have to go far—just half a mile or so.

"What happened?" I asked, as we slowed down in a patch of tall grass where four or five figures waited, silent shadows in the dim light. They were looking down at a prostrate form on the ground—Ling's body. I recognized Malpighi standing close by, and looked for Nieland. I didn't see him, but I couldn't spare more than a glance as I knelt beside Ling.

51

Some seconds dragged by before I realized that no one was answering my question.

I turned Ling over because he was lying face down. He was unconscious, but there seemed to be no sign of an injury to his body. Not until I felt the skin beneath his thick black hair did I realize that he had been hit on the side of the head. Hard.

I looked around. Malpighi had moved well away. Thayer was already raising my gun.

Strangely, I felt neither surprise nor anger. The realization that it was a trap came to me smoothly and coherently, clicking into place in my head like a piece from a jigsaw puzzle.

I hurled the medical bag at Thayer, but he had no trouble dodging it. The others raised their guns. There was nothing I could do—no earthly point in pretending that I could run or make a fight of it.

I looked at Malpighi, but he was too far away from the lamp for it to illuminate his face. Obviously, though, he knew what he was doing. This had been planned. Ogburn must be in on it too.

"Where's Nieland?" I asked.

"Behind a bush," said Malpighi. "He ain't dead. Gagged and tied. He'll get free easy enough. We ain't murderin' nobody."

"You've cracked Ling's skull," I said, not knowing whether it was true or not.

"He gave us a fight. Someone had to hit him. He's not dead. Where's the girl?"

The last question was addressed not to me but to Thayer.

"Wasn't there," said Thayer. "Maybe on the ship. We can take care of her later."

My mouth was dry.

"We'll put her ashore before we leave," said Malpighi. There was a note of relish in his voice—not because he was sadistically contemplating raping Mariel, but because he was in control and I couldn't do anything and he wanted me to know it.

"Where are you going to go?" I asked him.

"Home," he said. "We got water. We got all the rations

you piled up for your stay here. We don't need no roots or meat. We just want to get out of here. We don't see any reason why any more of us should get killed. You promised us a lot of money for this trip, but you didn't say nothing about people getting killed. We don't want to end up like the others—Verheyden and his crew. We're going home. Now."

"And when you get back home?" I said. "What do you tell them?"

"We tell them you all got carried off," he said. "You went out to look for natives an' you never came back. We waited, we hunted, but two of our best men were shot. There was a fight. We had to retreat or we'd ha' been slaughtered to a man. We'll make ourselves heroes. An' we'll collect our money, too."

I said: "Someone will talk. You lot don't like one another any better than you like us. Someone will blow the whole thing to spite someone else. Half of the poor sods don't know what's happening, do they? Just Ogburn and you, hey? You've left them all an excuse. It wasn't me, they'll say, it was Ogburn and Malpighi. I had to go along. Someone will say it. Someone always does. What's the penalty for a crime like this back in the colony, hey? But suppose Thayer there has a change of heart, Malpighi? Suppose he shoots you instead of me? He *can* be a hero. You can all be heroes, boys. Just shoot the right man. . . ."

I never thought it would work.

It didn't.

The dart took me in the shoulder. I tried to look over the shoulder to see where it had gone in, but the angle was impossible. I remained kneeling, waiting for the drug to black me out. I didn't try to fight it. I keeled over slowly. I didn't want to hurt myself, or make him fire again.

The world spun around me, like a black whirlpool, and I seemed to continue falling, through the ground . . . a long, long way.

8

I became slowly conscious of the fact that someone was slapping my face.

Under the circumstances, it seemed to be something of a lousy thing to do. It was taking advantage of my helplessness. I was a sick man, and very tired. I was also dreaming, and though the slaps were driving the substance of the dream away from the clutches of consciousness I had the strong impression that it had been a fairly pleasant dream.

I felt the collar of my one-piece gripped and my head was yanked from its resting place. I didn't seem to have any alternative but to wake up.

I woke up.

"Come on, Alex!" she was saying, through gritted teeth.

I looked at her, and remembered.

"Mariel!"

"Who were you expecting—the Virgin Mary?"

She let my head sink back to the ground. Beside me was a body. I rolled over, away from it, and got to my knees. I peered at Ling, and reached out to take his wrist. He was cold. The bastards *had* cracked his skull. I realized that it was still the middle of the night, but that Mariel was holding a bright lantern.

"Where's Nieland?" I asked.

"How should I know?"

"They said they left him behind a bush—tied up but loose enough to get free. They were very scrupulous about murder—at least, the way they talked. . . ." I remembered something else about the way they had talked. "How did you get here?" I asked.

"Followed the trail blazed on the trees," she replied.

"No, I don't mean how, I mean *how?* When I got shot you were scheduled for a gang rape. You don't *look* as if you've been raped. Or shot by anaesthetic darts."

54

"I was bringing the last of the stuff from the ship's hold," she said. "Lanterns and extra equipment—mostly spare stuff, but you weren't in a very good mood and I thought I might as well *pretend* to be useful. I met Ogburn. He offered to help me. I don't know what he said after that—I was too busy being scared of what he wasn't saying. I couldn't get back in time to warn you, so I just bluffed until Ogburn went back into his cabin. I got all the remaining food concentrates out of the hold and put them in the rowboat. Then I went to Nieland's cabin and took the navigational stuff. Then I went to the armory and got the remaining guns. The boat was a bit full by then so I dumped those over the side. I stole the needle from the compass. I would have drilled a couple of holes in the side or something, but I didn't have the time and I'd chucked the only remaining tools over the side with the guns.

"I got into the rowboat and started upriver. I had to lighten the load a bit more, so some of the heavy stuff went over, but I managed to get away all right. It was dark, of course, and the boat was moored on the far side of the ship, so no one could see what I was doing. I found a place to land and unloaded all the food and such into a crack in the rock. Then I pushed the boat out into midstream again so it would float back to the ship and maybe past it and all the way down to sea. I transferred the food bit by bit to the top of the slope, and then hid it in the trees.

"I sat tight for a while, then wormed my way back to see what was going on. They'd packed up for the night. I skirted the stockade and set off in the direction the foraging party had gone. There were no lights ashore, so I presumed there were no lookouts, and I put the lamp on low until I found a scored tree. Then I followed the trail, turning up the light as I came. I think we're safe, though—I'm pretty sure they're all back on the ship. They'll probably take off first thing in the morning . . . unless, of course, they start checking supplies."

"Jesus," I said, softly.

"The only problem is," she said, "what do we do next. We've got the bulk of the food—except for the stuff that had already come ashore—and we have some of your equipment, though not the most important stuff. We don't have any guns, and they have six plus your dart rifle. On balance, I'd say we're in a bit of a spot and so are they. They could navigate their way across the ocean without the instruments or the compass, but will they try without supplies they can trust? You've tested a lot of the local produce, but will they be able to make anything of your notes? I sure as hell never can."

I shook my head wonderingly.

"Let's get out of here," I said. "If they find out what you've done they'll come looking for us. They must have noticed your absence—we're just bloody lucky they haven't looked in the hold. We'd best make our way up-river. Get ourselves lost, for the time being. I'm not risking going back to the stockade."

I got up, and started looking round bushes. There was no sign of Nieland, but I did find a patch of squashed grass where he might have lain.

"Malpighi said he'd get loose," I muttered. "Damn fool must have tried to wake me, failed, and set off on his own. God only knows what he'll try to do. He surely won't have gone back to the stockade."

The possibilities, while not exactly endless, did not seem to warrant any more in the way of analytical commentary.

"Okay," I said, "let's go."

I took the lantern from her hand, and then grabbed her hand to make sure we stayed together.

We had gone some distance before I spoke again. "In your shoes," I said, "I'd have run."

"I wanted to get a little of my own back," she said. "They were very nasty thoughts that Ogburn was thinking."

"Did you have to throw *all* the guns over the side?" I asked.

"I thought you didn't approve of guns."

"They have their uses. But we'll get by. You did one hell of a job. I don't know how we're going to put Humpty Dumpty together again, but you did a hell of a job."

"I thought we could negotiate," she said. "We have the food."

"Yeah," I said, without enthusiasm. She'd got some of her own back on the crew, all right—and maybe a bit for me, too. But she hadn't quite marooned them as finally as they'd marooned us. And we both knew, deep down, that there wasn't a hope in hell of negotiating our way back home on the *New Hope*. Even if we patched up the quarrel and somehow gained a little leverage to preserve our lives during the long journey home it would be a long, long trip. Accidents can happen at sea. Not to mention stranger things.

As we made our way westward in the starry night, I couldn't quite see how we were *ever* going to get off Delta.

9

We didn't go far—just far enough to get ourselves thoroughly lost. We could always find ourselves again by heading back to the river. What mattered was that *they* shouldn't be able to find *us*.

We rested underneath a tree, not really intending to doze off—sleeping in subtropical forests can be dangerous. But the aftereffects of the drug made me far too drowsy to resist the pull of sleep, and I succumbed. I assume that Mariel must have done likewise, but at least she woke up when things began to happen.

I woke up when she began shaking my arm.

Day had dawned, and the cool morning was all about us. There was a heavy dew. There were also five aliens standing round in a semicircle contemplating our prostrate forms. I sat up very suddenly.

They were all males—one very large, the others in assorted sizes, presumably in varying stages of maturity. They were naked except for belts slung over their shoulders, with little pouches and pockets hung therefrom. The biggest one was carrying a spear with an iron blade. Two of the others had big knives, also of iron. All the ones with weapons were fingering them nervously while they watched us. Their fur was dark, with a pattern (black on brown) that was halfway between random blotches and vertical stripes. They looked like anthropomorphized versions of giant tabby cats.

The big male studied me carefully. He had dark brown eyes with wide pupils—not catlike pupils, but humanoid circular ones. He wrinkled his nose as if he didn't take too kindly to the way I stank. His lower jaw moved a little, as if he wanted to say something but couldn't think of an apposite remark.

Who could blame him?

I put up my hands, palms outward, to show that there

was nothing in them. The lamp lay beside me—I ignored it.

I got slowly to my feet.

The big one said something. The sounds he made were not unlike one of the more fluid human languages—Japanese, perhaps. But some consonants were missing, others blurred.

"I'm sorry," I said, inadequately. "I don't understand."

I looked down at Mariel, helplessly appealing for her to take over. This was her show. But as she struggled to her feet the big one ignored her. He said something else to me, in a tone that suggested he was asking a question.

"He's talking to you because you're the biggest," she said. I forgave her for not saying "bigger"—it was a stressful moment and she could be excused the slip.

"Look," I said, trying to sound pleasant and reassuring. "I wish I knew what you were talking about, but I don't. I can assure you, though, that I feel nothing but goodwill toward you and yours."

It wasn't much, but it beat *Me Alex, Who You?* He didn't look angry. I couldn't tell whether he looked puzzled or not—his brow wasn't built for furrowing.

He said something to the next in line, who answered monosyllabically. Then he said something else to me.

Affably, I said: "Don't just lie there, help me!" I didn't take my eyes off the alien while I said it.

Mariel said: "You're doing fine," and giggled. It didn't seem to me to be any time for merriment. I hoped that she wasn't showing her teeth—it's rumored that that's one of the most dangerous things to do when trying to chat to other species. Not that the guy who started the rumor had any practical experience in the matter.

Then the big one came to a decision. He dropped his spear, reached out his long furry arms and gripped both my wrists. The way he did it brought my own fingers round into contact with his wrists, and it seemed natural to join the clasp. I did. He let go a long sound that was half-way between a purr and a muffled war-whoop. The other four began chattering. The whole atmosphere seemed much more relaxed.

"Congratulations," said Mariel.

My new friend let got of my left arm but transferred grip on the other to take me by the elbow and guide me away. I let him guide me. Mariel picked up the lantern. One of the younger aliens picked up the leader's weapon. And off we went—heading west.

At the first opportunity, I asked Mariel what had happened.

"I'm not sure," she said. "They obviously decided that we're worth getting to know. They haven't captured us . . . they're just taking us home to meet the folks. What I can't understand is why the big one seemed so very *pleased* when he decided to be friends."

"You think he's seen humans before?"

"Maybe. I can't tell."

We were all walking as a group, now. All friends together, following our leader. I swapped curious glances with the younger aliens. They talked—presumably about us—and we talked about them. It was all very amicable. I had difficulty keeping it in mind that we didn't know what the hell was happening. It all seemed so *natural*.

"Well," I said, "you got your chance. Whatever else happens you met your aliens. You have time to get to know them. Maybe all the time in the world."

"Count your blessings," she said. "They're friendly. And they have fishing boats. It could be we've got a better chance of ultimately getting home than Ogburn's pirates."

"Whoever built that dhow," I said, "it wasn't this lot. These are swidden farmers . . . forest people. They migrate from place to place, burning out areas of forest and cultivating the ashy soil. They can only stay in one place for a couple of years—then the soil begins to become exhausted and they move on, letting the forest grow back. They aren't the kind of people who build boats."

"They aren't the kind of people who make steel, either," she said. "But look at those knives."

I looked at the knives carried by the younger men. I had assumed that they were beaten iron, but now they'd been called to my attention I saw that they were strangely smooth. Not rusted. Their edges looked good and sharp. I checked the spear that the big one had been carrying

60

when first we saw him. *That* was iron, and rusted. It had been hammered out, and carried no edge at all—just a blunt point.

"They trade," I said, stating what was now the obvious. "And what's more, they trade with someone who has a fairly sophisticated knowledge of metalwork."

"The dhow builders," she said.

I wondered. We had no dependable information about the accomplishments of the more civilized aliens to the north, but dhows and stainless steel struck me as being pretty advanced. More advanced than we could possibly have anticipated.

While we marched, they made no attempt to open communication. They didn't attempt to exchange names, or teach us words of any kind. But they talked to one another, and Mariel watched. I didn't expect her to begin picking up the language until they actually began to teach us, but I knew that when that time came she'd be all geared up to master it at superhuman speed. She'd know all the sounds, and she'd know the tones and the rhythms. It all came naturally to her. And learning it wouldn't be just a matter of memorizing the labels—not for her. She'd actually get to grips with the feelings behind it, the ways of thinking implicit in it. She had a very flexible world view, an elastic mind. It was the necessity of *keeping* that elasticity which really set the limit on her ability. Talents dwindle not for any of the quasi-supernatural reasons she'd quoted aboard the ship, but for the simple reason that children growing up inevitably settle into the world view of their own kind. Their minds crystallize out, their ways of thinking become fixed. If Mariel hadn't come out with the *Daedalus* she might already have lost her "gift of tongues." A ceaseless supply of new worlds and new cultures is one way to help maintain elasticity.

Despite the fact that the situation as a whole was clouded by every possible uncertainty, I couldn't help feeling glad that she had, whatever else might happen, got her chance with the natives of Delta.

10

We reached the village late in the day. It was in a little gully between two slopes, one of which was steep enough for bare rock to show through here and there. The rock had been worked by metal tools. There was a stream cutting through the gully, and they had built a small dam to contain a sizable pool at the lower neck of the cleft. There were about forty huts, made mostly from thin laths of wood, matted leaves that resembled fern or bracken, and mud-caked straw. There were a lot of small children and a lot of small animals running loose between the huts on the cleared, stony ground. The burnt-out enclaves where the various families cultivated their plots were scattered on both sides of the stream downstream of the village itself. There were two or three fires set close together in the center of the living area.

A great deal of curiosity was aroused by our arrival, but not much commotion. Everyone stared, but no one crowded close to get a better look at us. We went first to the pool, where our escorts drank their fill after a thirsty day's marching. We drank too, a little more modestly. The leader of our little group was approached by a group of natives his own size, and they indulged in an animate conversation. They were obviously discussing us, but there was no attempt at formal introduction.

"The one who made friends with us is trying to explain himself," said Mariel. "There doesn't seem to be one among the others who has special authority. If they have a chief, he's not out here. One or two of the others don't seem very pleased with him, but our friend is trying to mollify them. They don't seem particularly hostile to us—if I had to guess I'd say they want to know why he didn't follow through with whatever the original purpose of his expedition was. He's trying to tell them that we're more important."

As running commentaries go, it seemed fairly adequate.

Eventually, the one who'd brought us here came back, and began ushering us forward again. He took us to one of the huts and invited us inside. He made signs at us, which even I had no difficulty interpreting as instructions to stay put. Then he went back to his discussion group, to argue a bit more. I peered out of the doorway for a few minutes, watching the villagers, but after a while I got tired of being watched in turn. I went inside.

There wasn't much in the hut—two long mounds of straw, presumably used for sleeping; a few bowls carved out of wood—all empty and quite clean; a pot full of some greasy substance rather like soap. One of the inner walls, though, was sown with the colored feathers of a dozen different species of bird—just the wing feathers, obviously saved for some decorative purpose. And in little grass pockets built into the same wall there was an assortment of small tools—scrapers, knives, forks, even pairs of forceps. They were almost all made from wood or bone, but one or two were made from a horny substance that may have been from the bill of a bird. There was no metal at all.

"Home sweet home," I murmured.

The straw had a musty animal odor, but it wasn't too hard to get used to.

Mariel sat on the floor with the lantern in front of her, staring at it.

"I wish I'd brought some of the food," she said. "I could have loaded up a packsack."

"They'll feed us," I said. "It's safe to assume that anything they eat won't be poisonous to us. Poisons are fairly ubiquitous. And their bacteria certainly won't worry us except, perhaps, for a touch of gut sensitivity. Anyhow, we don't have a lot of choice."

About an hour passed before we had visitors. There were four of them, and I realized with a guilty start when they came through the door that I couldn't tell which of them, if any, was the one who'd brought us here. I'd kept my eyes on him before, but I couldn't actually *recognize* him. One of the four, however, I eliminated from consideration. He was wearing a headdress made out of feathers and bits of black fur. He seemed to be the one in command, but whether he was the tribal chief or the local shaman there was no way of knowing. He looked us both over very carefully. Then we all sat down, in an approximate circle, with the one in the headdress facing me. He asked questions. I tried to convey my inability to answer. He held conferences with the others. Then they asked more questions. I tried to tell them our names. They didn't get it—or refused to acknowledge it. One of them handed the lantern to the guy in the fancy headgear, who inspected it closely, figured out how to turn it on, and lit up the inside of the hut. He tested the transparent plastic for heat. I took it from him and showed him how to vary the intensity of both light and heat. Then I switched off, unscrewed the base and showed him the fuel cell. He took a lively interest in all of this, and didn't seem to attribute any of it to evil magic. In the end, I made a show of making him a gift of the lantern. He took it with apparent pleasure.

I felt that we were really getting somewhere, then. I tried again with our names, but again it didn't seem to click. I tried him with the word "lamp," and he tried to repeat that. He couldn't quite manage the *mp* sound because of his arched upper lip, but he made a useful attempt. In a fit of generosity I brought my penknife out of my pocket and made a gift of that, too. He played with both blades and tried to say "knife," making a better job of the word than he'd been able to do with "lamp." By the time he left, he seemed genuinely enthusiastic about the whole affair.

Mariel congratulated me again. They still hadn't taken much notice of her—presumably because she was smaller. I didn't suppose that the aliens could recognize her as obviously female.

We ate with the family shortly after our inquisitors had gone. We were invited out of the hut by a single male—I assumed it was the one who'd brought us in, but couldn't take an oath on it—and we squatted on the ground outside with him, a female, and two infants. We ate something like lukewarm sago from wooden plates, and then were offered some large grubs. With the best will in the world I couldn't summon up the courage, and we declined. It was a silent meal—they all seemed to accept that they couldn't talk to us, and our presence seemed to inhibit them. Afterward, we were politely ushered back into the hut.

"As a pattern for life," I said, "this could get boring."

"It's only temporary," she assured me. "I think they're starting a new building up near the top of the cleft. I saw a group of males haggling over something and making marks on the ground. It's probably the posh end of the village."

"For us?" It seemed like a nice gesture. "That's very nice of them. Generosity obviously pays."

"I think the one who came to look us over was the local wise man," she said. "The guy who's supposed to know the answers to all questions. He had to weigh us up, decide where we'd fit into the scheme of things. These people are savages—their philosophy of life hasn't got room for more things in heaven and earth than they habitually dream of. They have to work out a role for us, and he was the man with the job of doing it. You made a hit—so we're honored members of the community. For now. That's the way I see it."

It was pretty much the way I saw it, too. We had prestige, because we had the gifts of civilization—light and metal. They obviously had some source of supply of the latter, already worked into weapons. If they had to trade for them they probably got ripped off in no uncertain terms. We probably represented an alternative—a potential means of enriching the whole tribe. I wasn't exactly sure that I wanted to play Prometheus, but that seemed to be the part they had me down for. It was natural enough.

Much later, we had another visitor. Or, to be strictly accurate, an addition to our numbers. It was Nieland. He was brought in by a pair of males, looking quite terrified.

I'd never before seen anyone look so glad to see me. His relief was beyond words. He just sank down on the dirt floor, sweating profusely and looking thankful.

"They found you, then," I commented, airily, taking advantage of my familiarity with the situation.

65

"I thought you were dead," he said.

"You shouldn't have wandered off," I told him.

"I thought you were *dead*," he said, again. You were lying there with Ling—I thought they'd shot you both and left me to die. It was pitch dark except for the stars . . . I didn't find you until I fell over you. I had to get away . . . back to the river . . . I don't know where . . . I got lost. I was wandering about the forest all day, until. . . ."

"I think we can piece together the rest in our minds," I said. "Get some rest. It must have been a long walk—and these people can really cover the ground."

He did, in fact, look exhausted.

"Two chance meetings in one day," I said to Mariel in a worried tone. "Not likely."

"There weren't many males about the village when we were out having high tea," she mused. "Only the ones at the head of the valley. The rest may have had other things to occupy them. Or. . . ."

"They may have been out searching the forest for more miracle-workers from across the sea. And if they find the *New Hope*. . . ."

"They can hardly miss her."

"Our popularity might fail. . . very suddenly."

She nodded. "I think we'd better pray that they pulled up anchor this morning," she said.

"Without checking the hold?"

She shrugged. "They built up a fair hatred for this place. Verging on superstitious dread. They might have sailed regardless, reckoning on trying their luck elsewhere. They might decide not to try to get supplies from the forest at all. Men like Ogburn and Malpighi would be more likely to think of *stealing* supplies. They still have some guns— maybe they'll work their way north after the fishing boat you saw."

I turned to Nieland, who was slowly recovering his breath and his composure.

"What do you think?" I asked.

"I don't think they'll stay at the base," he said. "Not after what they did. They'll run, if only to get away from the scene of the crime."

It sounded plausible enough. But I still felt a little

66

uneasy. If the aliens *did* find our erstwhile companions, and approached them in optimistic friendship. . . .

But there was nothing we could do, either way. Nothing but wait.

11

The village did seem to get more crowded around dusk. People were coming in from all around, though whether they'd been searching for more humans or were simply about their own business, there was no way to tell.

When it grew dark, they built up the fires in the middle of the village, and they hammered a stake into the ground nearby. For a moment, I thought it might be an ominous sign, but with some ceremony they attached to its point the lamp I'd given to the wise man, and they turned its light up high. It glowed like a miniature sun, but whitely.

I watched them from the doorway as they admired the pure white light. It seemed to make quite an impression. Then somebody got out a drum and started beating it. Someone else joined in.

There are always drums in jungle melodramas. Sanders of the river was perpetually surrounded by ominous percussion and the feebler bearers of the white man's burden always used to get the jitters about restless natives. But this was dance music.

"I think there's a party starting," I said to Mariel. "But we don't seem to have been invited."

"We could always wander out," she suggested. "There's no guard on the door. We aren't prisoners."

I considered it. It was pretty dark in the hut, and none too comfortable. I knew that Nieland was apprehensive, but I was fed up with sitting around in the wings.

As I moved toward the light, where the whole tribe seemed to be gathering, the wailing started. To describe it thus is perhaps a little unfair, but it really wasn't an aesthetically pleasing sound. There was little that was melodious about the way these people spoke, and their singing was worse. Only one voice took the lead at any one time, but there were always a lot more muttering a kind of chorus, providing a rhythm without drowning out the soloist. The solo part was passed from voice to voice about every half-minute. Females took turns as well as males, but it was mostly the older members of the tribe who participated. Some of the children were dancing—each one alone and making it up as he or she went along, but almost everyone else was either sitting or kneeling in a great circle around the fires and the single lantern perched upon its pole.

There was nothing particularly solemn about what was happening—the ones who were kneeling weren't praying, just making themselves comfortable. We didn't push our way to the front, but sat down near the back. The aliens made room for us, and our neighbors stared at us covertly. They didn't seem surprised or resentful at our coming out to join them.

The song, I guessed, was the accumulated knowledge and tradition of the tribe, organized into units. No one had to know it all but everyone probably knew most of it. Any part might be taken by any of a dozen of the older members of the tribe, and even the children probably knew a few verses each. We listened in silence, understanding not a word. It wasn't beautiful, but it was fascinating, and the rhythm, though fast, was almost hypnotic. Maybe somewhere toward the end of the song they'd be making up new verses—verses about us. Something new to sing about.

I let myself be absorbed into the rhythm. I could almost feel that I belonged. I no longer felt frightened by the possibilities that still lurked within the situation. For the moment, it was all okay.

Suddenly, there was a movement to the left, and I looked up to see the alien in the feathered headdress and two companions picking their way through the crowd toward me. I stood up to meet him. The singing was still in progress, so he didn't attempt to speak, but he put out his hand in a beckoning gesture. Mariel still hadn't noticed, so I touched her shoulder. Nieland was already looking up.

I moved forward, and the other took my arm in his slender-fingered hand. I could feel blunt vestigial claws denting my skin.

He was exposing his teeth in what I took to be the beginning of a smile or a gentle laugh. I smiled back.

And he was pitched backward as if struck down by a giant hand.

Time seemed to congeal as he fell, arms akimbo, one of those vestigial claws catching briefly in my sleeve. He let go a sound that was only incipiently a scream.

Sticking out of his chest was a four-inch shaft, neatly feathered with slivers of wood.

I had just time to notice this before the howling started and all hell broke loose. Suddenly everyone was up and running, yelling like banshees.

I picked Mariel up from the floor and shoved her toward the hut from which we'd come. "Get under cover!" I shouted. I didn't bother looking around for Nieland—he could take care of himself. I followed Mariel as she sprinted for the shadows within the hut. But we were too late. Someone else was heading that way ahead of us—one of the females, presumably the one with whom we'd eaten earlier in the day. She was entitled—it was her hut—but she never reached it. Something else came out of the gap between the huts and struck her down with a savage sideways blow of what looked like a cutlass. It was an alien, and it looked just like any other alien to me, but *they* could tell the difference. A child running along beside me turned tail and ran in another direction.

I took the hint. I went sideways, pulling Mariel with me, not knowing where I was going but determined to get there fast. Another shadow yawned invitingly beside another hut, and I ran into it, making my way along the outer wall and round the back. Once there I tried to keep going straight out into the jungle, but I had forgotten the walls of the cleft. I ran straight into a rock face, and cursed loudly. I flattened myself up against the rock and began to feel my way along. Mariel was still with me, keeping her hand in touch with my arm though not actually gripping it. Five or six meters along the ragged face I found vegetation again, and realized that what I'd run into was an outcrop. There was a triangular gap behind

70

it—not exactly a hiding place, but at least somewhere out of the way.

I moved into it, pulling Mariel behind me. We stood stock still, listening. We could see nothing—foliage above our heads cut out most of the stars and the huts blocked out the light of the lantern and the fires.

The screaming was still going on, and we didn't need to speak the language to appreciate the mixture of panic-stricken yells of terror and the whoops of the marauders. Through it all I could feel the beat of my heart, pounding like a hammer.

"We've got to make a run for it," hissed Mariel. "It sounds like a massacre."

There was no direct evidence of which way the battle was going, but whoever was attacking had had everything in their favor. They had had plenty of time to group their forces and they had picked the moment. Our lot hadn't had their arms ready to hand, and they weren't exactly well-supplied with weaponry. I didn't want to start running around blind, but I didn't want to hang about and wait for the butchers.

"Okay," I whispered. I began to creep along parallel with the wall of the cleft, toward the lower end of the village and the dam.

I knew that there was something of a bottleneck at the pool, but figured that if we could get through it we'd be away, with nothing but an infinite sea of trees in front of us. But there was no way I could move silently through the vegetation, and if there was anyone in that bottleneck. . . .

Step by step we moved forward, futile eyes searching the darkness.

There was a small sound, very close at hand. A scratching sound. As the thought leapt into my mind that I *knew* that sound it was instantly confirmed. A match flared into life. . . .

And the yellow glow illuminated the furred face of an alien who must have been all of seven and a half feet tall. His bright brown eyes caught the light of the match and seemed to gleam like gold. I saw the mouth open to reveal the pointed teeth.

I aimed a kick at where I thought his groin might be, and he gasped as my boot hit his thigh. Reflexively, he reached out a long, long arm and shoved me back. The match didn't go out, and I saw his mouth move to let go a spitting hiss and then a clicking sound. I put up my hand to shield my face, knowing as I did so that it was hopeless. Mariel, behind me, gasped out the ghost of a scream.

"Blurry iriot," hissed a voice. "S'ay s'ill."

For a second or two, I just couldn't believe that it was the alien who had spoken. I had seen his mouth move, but it just didn't seem possible. The accent was atrocious, but the words were unmistakable. I just froze, completely confused.

It was, when all was said and done, what he'd asked of me.

The frail light flickered in his hand, and he turned the match to keep it alight. He lowered it slightly, so that it illuminated his body. That, too, was a shock. For one thing, he was wearing clothing. Not much, but enough—a sleeveless tunic of some leathery substance, and a short skirt or kilt of dark blue cloth. He had a belt around his waist with a wicked-looking knife tucked neatly into a scabbard. What was even more astonishing was the thing that he carried in his other hand. It was a crossbow, about four feet long from stock to head with a three-foot bow. There was a quiver of bolts slung across his shoulder. He was, to coin a phrase, armed to the teeth.

Somewhere behind us, one of the huts went up in flames. Its matted wall and dry roof went up very rapidly. By the light of the flames we could see somewhat more than by the light of the match, which now expired. Standing behind the alien who'd stopped us were two more silent figures, impassively waiting.

One of them was an alien, similarly dressed but carrying only a heavy wooden club.

The other was a human. He was a little shorter than I, thinly built, with light brown hair and eyes which caught the firelight in the same way as the alien's had. He was looking straight at me, with his face set hard in a grim half-smile. He didn't seem surprised to see me.

72

"Okay," said the one who'd struck the match. "All okay. S'ay cool. All o'er soon."

"What the hell are you *doing*?" I whispered. I had a hundred questions, but that one took precedence.

"Saving you from the savages," said the human. His voice was dry and flat. I couldn't tell whether it was a simple statement or whether he was being sarcastic. His eyes were still on my face, staring with the same kind of fascination that I had seen in a dozen pairs of alien eyes during the day.

"They hadn't harmed us," I whispered. "They were friendly. We weren't in any danger."

The human shook his head. "Forest savages," he said.

"Stop it!" I said, abandoning the whisper for a normal tone. "If you started this, for God's sake stop it."

He looked over my shoulder then. Several more huts had been fired, and there was now a great deal of light illuminating his face. I turned to look as well. The sound was dying, and so was the fight. The figures which were moving in the clearing now were all clothed, though some had loincloths instead of skirts, and some had shirts of lighter material instead of the leathery waistcoats. I couldn't see any of the forest people except for those lying dead on the ground, who included males, females and children.

"The rest have run into the forest," said the dry voice. "It's all over now. You're safe."

I saw two figures coming toward us, silhouetted against the fire. One was tall and thin, the other short and stocky. Nieland had been "saved" too.

"S'okay," said the alien who'd lit the match. "We on yur si', see."

I looked back at the human. "Who are you?" I demanded.

"My name's Verheyden," he replied. "Jan Verheyden. This is Al'ha."

The alien with the crossbow dropped the weapon, catching it between his legs, and stuck out his hand. "Pleas'a meetya," he said.

Too dazed to think straight, I took his hand and let him shake mine.

"I'm Alexis Alexander," I said. "But you don't *understand*. We weren't being held captive. They didn't mean us any harm."

Jan Verheyden, still poker-faced, simply shrugged his shoulders.

"What does it matter?" he said. "Forest savages."

Al'ha let go of my hand. "Savages," he echoed, as if that explained everything.

I realized that they very probably *did* understand. They just didn't care. To them, the savages were just vermin. Al'ha looked just like they did—even the pattern on his fur, what I could see of it, was indistinguishable from theirs. But he, like the alien who'd cut down the female as we tried to reach the hut, had no difficulty in drawing distinctions.

I felt the anger ebbing away within me, because it was helpless to find any expression.

I watched the expression of utter surprise on Nieland's face as he came face to face with Jan Verheyden. He had had one hell of a day for surprises. Still, he had built the *New Hope* to come in search of adventure. He was getting a damn good run for his money.

"What now?" he said, in a tone that had gone beyond bewilderment.

I looked from his face to Verheyden's, and back again.

What now, indeed? I wondered.

12

"*Ilah'y'su* is anchored at a small village on the coast," said Jan Verheyden. "This is about as far south as we come, trading finished cloth and metal implements for raw materials—mostly oil from various seabeasts. There are some deep wells in the seabed offshore there and the local fisherman build ramps from the shore to catch them entirely without boats. Incredible. They have a lot of trouble with the savages—they're always squabbling and raiding one another. A dhow had brought news farther north that a big ship had been seen here, but it wasn't until the villagers claimed to have seen it that I really took it seriously. We didn't know how far south you'd sailed, and we couldn't take *Ilah'y'su* south because some of the cargo's perishable. But we came inland hunting, and some of the trackers from the village picked up your trail where the savages found you this morning. We found your camp, but the ship had already sailed. We picked up your own trail again but it got dark while we were still following. Attacking seemed the logical thing to do. You're very lucky. If we hadn't found you, you'd have had damn little chance of reaching civilization, whether the savages were friendly or not. And you can't trust the savages. We've had trouble with them in the west, in the south . . . everywhere."

We were sitting in one of the few huts that hadn't been burnt out. We had re-possessed the fuel-celled lamp. The alien I'd given it to didn't need it any more, and his tribe—what was left of it—had scattered into the forest. There were just the five of us—we three "rescued" and our two chief rescuers: Jan Verheyden, captain of the good ship *Ilah'y'su*, and his towering right-hand man Al'ha. The rest of the attacking party had been a mixed bunch of aliens from the coastal village and Verheyden's crewmen.

There were a thousand things that I wanted to know, but I found difficulty in knowing where to start.

Jan Verheyden seemed tense and unsure of himself now. His voice was still deliberately flat and emotionless, but I could see now the anxiety that put pressure on the facade. Our arrival was at the root of that unease, but I wasn't quite sure why.

"Bernhard Verheyden must have been your father," said Nieland, saving me from the worry of not knowing where to start.

"That's right," said Jan.

"What happened to the *Floreat?*"

"She was wrecked. A long way north of here. Only eight got away in one of the boats. Two died within a day of reaching shore. My father, my mother . . . and four others . . . lived. They're all dead now. My father died early last year."

"And now you're alone?"

"No," he said, slightly surprised by the question. "There are five of us. Four brothers and a sister. Piet's the eldest, Charles and Christian are younger than me, and Anna is between them. We're carrying on his work. Piet took over even during the last year of his life . . . he was ill for a long time. . . ."

I noticed a curious thing while Jan was answering Nieland's questions. He kept glancing away, not because of any embarrassment or confusion, but because there was something in the room that continually attracted his attention, drawing his gaze again and again. It was the lantern.

I touched it with my fingertips. "Is it too bright?" I asked. "Or would you like me to turn the heat up a little?"

He shook his head. "That came from Lambda?" he asked, tentatively.

I realized why he had been puzzled. "Oh!" I said. "No. It comes from Earth."

His facade slipped at last as his face showed total astonishment. "From Earth!" he said, as if the words had been ripped unwillingly from his mouth.

"I'm sorry," I said, feeling a little pleased by the fact

that I'd set him back on his heels. "I should have introduced myself more fully. I came here with a ship—a support ship to give help to the colonies. Mariel is also from Earth."

His eyes flashed back to Nieland. "I'm from Lambda," said Nieland. "I built the ship—the *New Hope*—to follow in your father's footsteps. I thought it important that someone else should try to do what your father tried to do. I'm desperately sorry that it took such a long time. We couldn't know, you see, that anyone had survived. We *should* have begun again sooner, but perhaps you know something of the colony's difficulties."

He looked at us all with new eyes now, and it seemed to me that he looked considerably more favorably at Nieland than at Mariel or me. He had been prepared to take everything about us for granted, just to maintain his own sense of being totally in control of the situation. But now there were questions he had to ask.

"What happened to your ship?" he asked, of Nieland. "Why should they sail away this morning? Are they coming back?"

Nieland blushed. He seemed to lose his voice for a moment. "They . . . mutinied," he croaked. Then, recovering his normal tone, he went on: "We're stranded here. Just as you were . . . are. The *New Hope* has gone. . . ."

He was about to continue still further, to explain about the small matter of ship's supplies or the lack of them, but Mariel suddenly cut in with a question: "Your *Ilah*. . . ." She stumbled over the name and gave up. "Is she capable of crossing the ocean?"

I was surprised at first that she'd interrupted—it wasn't her style at all. It leapt to mind that she'd had some reason for not letting on that the *New Hope* might not have gone far. The fleeting notion was pushed aside, though, when Jan Verheyden answered that question with which she'd intervened.

"She's a good ship," he said. "A little smaller than the *Floreat*, carrying a little less sail . . . but I'd be prepared to tackle the ocean in her. I. . . ."

He stopped, suddenly. He had answered the question as

77

if it were a purely hypothetical one challenging the competence of his ship, and had been quick to defend her. But he realized now that it wasn't a hypothetical question, but a strictly practical one.

"Then you could take us home!" exclaimed Nieland. He was missing the point, too.

"You haven't tried to return to the colony?" I prompted, gently. The question was rhetorical, but it subtly invited him to provide an answer, if he was so inclined.

His face became firm again. He exchanged a glance with Al'ha, who sat patiently listening.

"Ak'lehr is my home," he said. "The Ore'l are my people. This is the only world we know."

"And your father?" asked Mariel, probing deep into the heart of the matter, as she saw it. "Didn't he want to return?"

"No," said Jan, flatly. "Never for a single moment."

"I don't understand," said Nieland.

Jan stood up, suddenly. His voice changed again, this time to the voice of command. "No more questions now," he stated. "We must all sleep. You three may have this hut. I'll sleep with my men. In the morning, we return to *Ilah'y'su*. We must return to Ak'lehr without further delay. I have a cargo that must travel immediately."

"We have to return to the camp first," I said.

"Why?" he demanded.

"For one thing," I said, "I had some valuable equipment there, and I want it back, if the mutineers haven't stolen or destroyed it." I didn't bother to list the second reason, which was that I wanted to pick up the stuff Mariel had stashed away upstream of the camp.

"All right," said Jan. "But we must not delay long."

With that, he went out. Al'ha followed him.

Nieland was about to complain once again that he didn't understand, but I waved him into silence.

"What's it all about?" I asked Mariel.

"I'm not entirely certain," she said. "But I'll start at the beginning. He was lying when he told that story about hunting. They came out here looking for the *New*

78

Hope—and they cut across the land because they didn't want to advertise their presence sailing up the river in a big ship—they couldn't even have approached unseen in a canoe. That was a direct lie. He wasn't directly lying when he talked about rescuing us from the forest people, but he wasn't exactly telling the truth either. He was— how shall I put it?—removing us from their charge, for safety's sake. He's glad the *New Hope*'s gone, and it'll help him be glad if he doesn't know she's coming back. You noticed that he wasn't exactly happy to learn that we come from Earth. That was an unexpected complication so far as he's concerned, but I'm not exactly sure what it complicates. I suspect he fears that there may be more men from Earth buzzing around his ears looking for us. It might be as well if we forgot to reassure him on that point.

"There was a tremendous emotional rush when he was asked about his father wanting to go home. It was a very touchy subject—but he wasn't lying when he said "Never." How we interpret that I'm not sure, but I think that there was some big argument among the survivors of the wreck. *Some* of them wanted to go home. But Ver- heyden—the father that is—probably overruled them. Maybe even prevented them. If you want my advice, we should all keep quiet about the matter of returning to Lambda. Because he isn't going to like the idea. Whatever his reasons are for staying there, they're strong."

"In a nutshell," I said, "we weren't prisoners before we were rescued, but we are now."

"We could be," she confirmed, "if we were prepared to make an issue of it."

"You think we ought to play along with the game?"

"What game?" interrupted Nieland, with sudden exas- peration. "What's going on here?"

He was completely at sea. He didn't know about Mariel's talent. It wasn't something we tended to adver- tise. Someone with a sensitivity to the meanings that lie behind other people's words is very useful, but it's rather undiplomatic to announce her presence.

"Come on," I said. "This is weird—you must see that.

We aren't out of trouble by a long way. Out of the frying pan and into God knows what. Jan Verheyden may be human, but that doesn't make him into our guardian angel in this heathenland. Ogburn was human, too. Jan isn't exactly overjoyed to have us here—he rescued us ... or snatched us, if you take a less benevolent view ... because given that we're already here he wanted us under *his* control. Giving us a lift back to Lambda is the last thing on his mind."

"But why?" asked Nieland, helplessly.

"We have plenty of time to find out," I said. "But if I had three guesses I know what number one would be. Jan's father, having been cast away here, decided to make the best of things. He had a lot to offer the aliens, if only he could persuade them that he was worth listening to. He's been empire-building. He's been playing fairy godmother. For thirty-seven years he's been stage-managing a technological revolution here. And now he's dead his children have taken over. Don't you see what an opportunity was presented to him here? An emergent civilization in the north—a whole continent in which to expand. It's Lambda in reverse. All the problems that Lambda has are meaningless here. There's no problem of co-adaptation, no manpower shortage. The only thing the aliens lack is the only thing that Lambda has—know-how. The knowledge to exploit the resources they must have already found. After a life of frustration in the colony, think what potential the alien culture must have offered to him!"

Nieland shook his head. "I can understand that," he said. "He was stranded here. He must have known there'd be no new ship for a long time—he probably believed that it would be never. So he helped the aliens to develop their resources. There's nothing wrong in that. But why, when it was possible to come home, did he decide to stay? And why this suspicion and hostility on the part of his son?"

"Guilt," said Mariel. "Just guilt. Bernhard Verheyden probably felt that in doing as he did he was in some way turning traitor. Perhaps he felt resentment against the colony—that would be easy enough, as you must know.

Half the people on Lambda thought that you were mad and dangerous. They resented your appropriation of resources to build the *New Hope*. It was probably no different in his day. When he cast his lot with the aliens he must have seen it as a total break. The guilt and the resentment fed one another, building in his mind to an iron-clad determination. And that's what he's passed on to his children. There's hatred in Jan—simple hatred. For the colony, for humankind. He didn't get that from the aliens. He can only have got it from his parents. He doesn't want to have anything to do with the colony. Most of all, he doesn't want the colony to know what he's doing—he and his brothers and sister. He's closed his mind so that all it contains is Delta, and everything outside it is . . . well, simply *outside*. He's not quite sane, you know. Not by our standards."

Nieland digested all this. He didn't challenge it, though he plainly doubted it. I didn't—I trusted Mariel well enough to know that she didn't make wild guesses. It was all conjectural, but it had to make sense in terms of what she'd read through Jan's words. Her talent was as powerful as ever. Nieland couldn't know that, but the very sureness of her words pressed him back into a corner. He had nothing to put in place of the story she'd constructed.

"In that case," he said, in an anxious voice, "what happens now?"

"That depends on Jan. He's taking us back to wherever-it-was . . . the capital city of the nation. Presumably it's not entirely his decision. I don't know whether his elder brother is in charge or whether the five function as a mini-democracy, but either way it isn't all down to Jan. We'll have a chance to make them see our kind of reason. And if not. . . ."

"Well?"

I shrugged. "How should I know? We join the gang, maybe. We hijack a ship. We hijack the empire. We get cast into a dark dungeon for the rest of our natural lives. There's only one thing certain, as far as I can see."

"And what's that?"

"If we're right," I said, "and Papa Verheyden really has given the aliens the benefit of everything he knew—

which must have been quite a lot—then this alien empire has a very bright future. And if, in the fullness of time they *do* decide, for reasons of their own, to pay a visit to Lambda . . . they'll go as conquerors."

13

In the morning, I got the first real opportunity to judge the extent of the carnage.

It was a pretty sickening sight. The attackers had cleaned up a little during the night. They'd collected the bodies and thrown them all into one of the huts before setting it aflame. The hut had gone up like a torch, but the mass of dead flesh inside hadn't gone up with it—the dry grass and wood and leaves had just burned on top of them. The corpses were charred, but still recognizably corpses. Mostly adults, but some children as well. Maybe thirty in all. About a third of the total population of what had been a village. I didn't bother to ask how many "civilized" aliens had been lost. Maybe one or two . . . maybe none at all. I watched the victors moving about the ruins the next day. They seemed quite oblivious to what was around them.

Forest savages, in their estimation, were less than nothing. In themselves, they were probably as friendly as the forest people. They probably thought of themselves as good and reasonable people. But their ideas ran in fixed channels and pre-set categories. Had I told them that in my eyes all of their species were alike they wouldn't have been able to understand.

We marched to the camp in a long, trailing crocodile. Jan was at the head, and he showed no particular interest in having us nearby. We joined the train in the middle, with aliens who couldn't speak English before and behind.

"Tell me about Bernhard Verheyden," I asked of Nieland.

He looked at me dubiously. "I was in my early twenties when the *Floreat* was launched," he said.

"You weren't exactly a babe in arms," I said. "And it *is* a small world. You must have known about him, even

83

if you never actually exchanged two words. You must have formed an opinion."

"He was a man of determination," said Nieland cautiously. "I admired him. So did my friends. Yes, others hated him. There were those who saw his ideas as a danger to the colony. They didn't think we could afford to build big ships for sailing round the world . . . they always said that: sailing round the world . . . he was sometimes an angry man. I heard him speak once or twice. He cursed the farmers for their narrow-mindedness, resented the control they had over the decisions of the councils. If only he *had* been granted more power . . . I always thought that perhaps he might have dragged us up out of the mud into which we were slowly sinking. He had other projects in mind—not just the ship. In fact, the ship was something of a last resort. . . ."

"And the reason that they yielded to him," I said, taking up the thread, "was—at least in part—to get him out of the way. To get the thorn out of their side."

"A few," he said, defensively. "There were some who said that."

"Did they say it about you, too?"

He looked down at the ground where he walked. "No," he said. "I don't think so. I was never a thorn. Not as he was. I was . . . singleminded, I suppose. I believed in the *New Hope*—largely, I think, because it was what *he* had finally succeeded in doing. It seemed to symbolize his enthusiasm, his determination . . . his passion."

These words came slowly, as if wrung from him against his will. Perhaps he hadn't thought about it before, and was only just realizing that his motives were mixed in that particular way.

"Good," I murmured. "Couldn't be better."

"What?"

"Someone has to talk to the Verheydens," I said. "To Jan—to all of them. It can't be me, or Mariel. We're from Earth—we're the unknown factor in the problem. But you could make them see reason, if you try. You can talk to them about their father. You can win their confidence. You can make them see that they have to make contact with the colony again. Now. An amicable contact, beneficial to both sides."

He looked at me, uncertainly. "I'm not sure . . ." he began.

"You have to," I reiterated. "Somebody has to make them see sense . . . and there's only us to do it. You can get close to them. I can't."

All he would say—unhappily—was "I'll try."

With the best will in the world, I couldn't muster a lot of confidence in him. His diplomatic record wasn't good. One adventure, one mutiny.

I wasn't surprised to find when we reached the stockade that nothing could be salvaged from within. They had packed up and taken everything, including all the equipment that had actually come ashore. But the little treasure-trove that Mariel had stashed away was undisturbed. Most of it consisted of packs of food concentrate, but among the spare equipment that had been in storage were some medical supplies, nearly a hundred fuel cells, a small optical microscope and attendant micro-instruments, and some photographic equipment. Not exactly a survival kit supreme, but all well worth having.

Jan Verheyden looked the stuff over with some interest, but showed no disposition to appropriate any of it. He even lent us a couple of his crewmen to help us carry it all.

We didn't waste much time resting before we began the long cross-country trek back to Jan's ship. He was impatient to get back home—not so much because he was worrying about his perishable cargo but because he wanted to share his problems with his kindred. His curiosity, though, made him relent his earlier determination to stay away from us, and he invited us to join him at the head of the column.

"You say that you came here in a ship whose purpose is to support the colonies," he said to me, initiating the line of inquiry which he most wanted to pursue.

"That's right," I confirmed.

"My father said that there would never be support from Earth. He said that one of the reasons the colonists were so determined to defend what they had rather than

85

trying to improve matters was that most of them half believed that help would come from Earth and that they only had to wait. But he said that Earth could not afford to send ships to help established colonies."

"It took a long time," I said. "But now we are contacting the colonies again. With the help that we can provide I'm confident that we can solve most of the colony's problems and set it on the road to progress once again."

All that was, of course, true. I didn't feel compelled to add that the *Daedalus* mission might be one of a kind. Let him assume whatever he wanted to about the kind of contact we had made, and the kind of help we might supply.

"Why did you come to Delta?" he asked.

"Another part of our purpose is to discover what contact has been made—or might be made—with alien races on the three colonized worlds which have intelligent indigenes. One of the things we have to report back is the progress that has been made in alien/human relationships on the various worlds. We thought that there would be little to report back about Attica, but sailed on the *New Hope* thinking that we might be able to help with an initial contact ourselves. It seems that we were mistaken."

"Report back?" he queried.

"To the UN," I explained. "They have to decide on the nature of the future space program. They have to plan carefully. What they decide depends very much on the kinds of situations we find."

I let him draw his own inferences from that, too—knowing that they would be all the wrong ones. Let him think that this world had come under the eagle eye of Earth, and that he might have to answer for anything that happened here to a higher authority. I knew that Nieland was listening carefully to what I was saying, and hoped that he wouldn't confuse the situation by adding more information—though even he knew little enough about the true situation.

"It is a long journey back to Ak'lehr," said Jan. "It will take eight or nine days. That is perhaps as well—there are some things you must know about the kingdom and its people. It is essential that you should put yourselves under our guidance. We know how to deal with the Ore'l

86

and you do not. In the capital there are political situations which need very careful handling. Piet will explain them fully, but I will do my best to prepare you."

Now *I* had to play the game of drawing inferences. It wasn't an even game, because I could always consult Mariel about the thoughts that lay behind his words, but even without that help I could see what he was getting at now. When in Rome, we had to do as the Romans did—we had to place ourselves under the "guidance" of the Verheyden family. If it should prove that they had to treat us with kindness and respect, and if circumstances were eventually to force them to send us home, then we must report back what they wanted us to report back. Jan obviously thought that he and his brethren could control the situation, even if their affairs couldn't be kept secret any more.

And since he and his brothers and sister were the only ones who could speak the alien language, and could thus control our negotiations with the natives, he was probably right.

"We're entirely in your hands," I assured him. "It makes our job much easier if contact has already been made—and productively made. I'd say that you seem to have made a very good start here in putting human/alien relationships on a friendly basis. I see no reason why we shouldn't be able to submit a very favorable report on the Attican situation in general."

That was laying it on a bit thick, but it had the desired effect. He stopped himself looking startled, and looked gratified instead.

"I think your father and yourselves have worked wonders," I said. "I look forward to seeing what you've achieved in the capital city."

I could have gone on to talk about the foundations of a mutually beneficial relationship between Ak'lehr and the colony, but I thought it best to introduce him to that possibility slowly.

With luck, I could talk the whole family into realizing that they could be hailed as heroes if they'd only accept that their mission in life was what *we* wanted to see rather than the way they saw it. With a lot of help from Nieland,

I thought, we might even persuade them to *believe* that what they'd been doing all along was what we wanted them to do. If only we could overcome the attitudes that Bernhard Verheyden had planted in their minds. . . .

"You seem to know a great deal about what we've done for the Ore'l," said Jan, suspiciously.

"We were talking about it last night after you left us," I said, disarmingly. "We've seen stainless steel knives, a fishing boat of advanced design, crossbows . . . and you obviously have a fine ship if it's capable of an ocean crossing. The aliens couldn't have done any of this without help. It all adds up to a wonderful achievement."

Flattery, in my experience, will get you almost anywhere.

"Yes," he said. "Yes, it is." There was satisfaction in his tone.

There was a brief, awkward silence while he built up the impetus to change the subject. Eventually, he said: "What happened last night in the village . . . you disapprove of what we did . . . you don't think it was necessary to attack the savages."

Knowing that it was dangerous ground, I decided that the truth was best.

"It was a massacre," I said. "They didn't mean us any harm."

"Do you understand *why* they didn't mean you any harm?"

I frowned. "What do you mean?"

"They knew about humans," he said. "Rumor travels . . . even this far south. They had knives that were made in the capital—magic things, it must have seemed to them. I don't know whether they stole them or traded for them, but either way they associated them with us. When they found you, you see, they thought that you were a gift from their ancestors. They thought you'd been sent to give them all the wonderful things that we'd given to the men of the north. That's why they welcomed you . . . and they'd never have let you go. *Never.* We had to do what we did. You must see that."

I knew that he was talking sense. It hadn't occurred to me to explain what had happened to us that way, but now he showed me, I realized that it was almost certainly true. A massacre is still a massacre, and the way that he and his companions had done it all so callously and so carefully still made me slightly sick, but he was asking me for reassurance, and I had to give it to him. I had to declare myself on his side.

"I see," I said.

"They *were* savages," he said. "Just stupid savages."

I gritted my teeth, and subdued the tremor of nausea in my stomach.

"Yes," I said. "I suppose they were."

In such ways are great alliances made . . . compacts that might save worlds.

14

As I had recently spent more than three months at sea the nine-day journey north along the coast of what I came to think of as the Ak'lehrian Empire was a pretty tiresome experience. The accommodation problem was even worse than aboard the *New Hope,* with Mariel and me sharing a cupboard with two bunks mounted one atop the other and Nieland sleeping on the floor of Jan's cabin.

I cannot say that Jan learned to trust us, but as time wore on his fears and suspicions seemed to decline. He accepted the new situation and seemed prepared to take things as they came. I didn't mention the possibility of an early return to Lambda, and I steered well clear of any potentially embarrassing questions about his father's motives and those of his family. I just accepted what he told me of their influence upon the empire and was always ready to be impressed. Jan, in turn, became free with information about the city of Ak'lehr and the political situation within the expanding horizons of the empire. The one aspect of his uneasiness which remained had nothing to do with the general aspects of the situation, but was a simple and straightforward discomfort in Mariel's presence. The reason for his nervousness was very simple. In all his life, he had known no human female save for his mother and his sister. I dismissed this slight problem from my mind as something of no importance. Perhaps I was wrong to do so.

From conversations held during the nine days I managed to piece together a reasonable skeleton account of Bernhard Verheyden's adventures in the land of the Ore'l. At the time of the shipwreck he had been nearly forty years old. Jan always referred to his mother as his father's wife, but it seemed that they had become "married" only after reaching Delta. The woman had been a crew member—effectively, leaving euphemism aside, one of the ship's whores. The survivors of the wreck, minus the two who'd died almost immediately, were brought by the fishermen who found them to a town, where they had been fed and rested, and ultimately taken over by the local scholars—who were also priests. Having been taken under the wing of the church Bernhard Verheyden and his companions were ultimately brought to the headquarters of the church's hierarchy in the city of Ak'lehr itself.

The city was in a geographically privileged position, in a strip of land between two rivers, and it had proved an ideal focal point for the steady growth of civilization along the banks of both, using agricultural methods based on the irrigation of the land by means of ditches and canals. Even at the time the survey team had been scanning the northern temperate zone of Delta from the air the food surpluses generated by this agricultural system had permitted something of a population explosion, which had resulted in the rapid expansion of Ak'lehrian culture in the interim. The population explosions generated by food surplus tend to create new categories in society: large armies, a thriving merchant class, and an abundant priesthood. The civil service—the administrators of the political entity that Ak'lehr's empire became—were supplied by the priesthood, who were qualified by virtue of their literacy. Although Ak'lehr had a supreme ruler, all the real power lay with the priesthood and the army. Even the king was held to be the earthly incarnation of the divine will, and was thus sanctioned in his rule by the church and perpetually subject to their interpretation of his role.

By the time Bernhard Verheyden arrived in Ak'lehr the aliens were already embarked upon an era of technological innovation. They had had the plow for some time, but had recently invented the seed-hopper and were making much more effective use of domestic animals as animal husbandry became a business and—slowly—a science. They had distinguished two varieties of their staple crop (a prolific grain whose seed tasted not unlike rice) which ripened early in the year and late in the year. They had also imported large quantities of leguminous plants into the heartland of the empire in order to revitalize the soil periodically. They were in the process of domesticating fruit trees and various species of root vegetable. Their yields were increasing year by year as their population increased. Eventually, the expansion curves would cross as the yield curve flattened out while the population curve tended evermore to the vertical, but for the time being they were secure. Verheyden had the knowledge to maintain them in that security for at least an extra century.

There was one thing in his favor that I put down to sheer good fortune. It was true that he had arrived in Ak'lehr at an opportune moment in terms of historical development, but at *any* stage he would still have had a great deal to offer in terms of technological know-how. The thing that really allowed him to assume a position of such influence, and which allowed him to *apply* what he knew directly to the social world of the Ore'l, was the nature of Ak'lehrian theology. Had the church which found him and took him in been an anti-materialistic salvation religion with a rigid dogma and table of laws Verheyden would have stood no chance of gaining any influence over the history of the empire. He would almost certainly have been perceived as dangerous and destroyed. But the church which he found had become organized only recently. It had not yet rigidified around a body of dogma. It had cooperated in—and had been a major factor in encouraging—the beginning of civilization and the years of plenty which had come from progress in mastery of the environment.

The Ak'lehrians had one god, but were not precisely monotheistic. Other tribes and cultures had other gods, they knew, and they did not assume either that these gods were false or were their own worshipped under another name. They merely held that their god was the best god, and that this superiority would be proved by the benefits which he bestowed upon his people. These benefits were easy enough to see. As Ak'lehr extended its dominion by conquest the priests followed the armies, and pointed out to the defeated tribes how much more there was to be gained from worshipping the Ak'lehrian way. It was an offer that was hard to refuse, especially as the army encouraged conversion in a number of unsubtle ways. Ak'lehr had its fair share of the poor and the desperate, but there were always other peoples—real and imaginary—which could be cited by the priests as evidence that the Ak'lehrian poor were far better off than they might otherwise be. (And, in any case, it was the rich who really supported the church—and they were *obviously* reaping the rewards of god's favor).

Whereas the worshippers of a different kind of deity would have murdered Verheyden and his companions on the spot, the worshippers of Ak'lehr's god—Y'su—made him welcome. When they discovered that he had knowledge which they lacked—and proved it to them—they were in no doubt as to the reason why he had been washed up on their shores: he was *Ilah'y'su,* a messenger of god. Such became his title . . . and, of course, it was after him that Jan Verheyden's ship was named.

And so Bernhard Verheyden had begun a career of miracles. He had come to the aid of a metal-working industry which had been stretched to the limit of its resources for generations with the blast-furnace and with electroplating. He had shown the priesthood the limitations of their ideographic language and had introduced a phonetic variety of their own tongue as well as English. He had shown them electricity and the internal combustion engine. For ten or twelve years he had been active, traveling all over the heartland of the empire, building the machines that he wanted to give to the empire, working with blacksmiths and craftsmen. Then he had realized that progress was too slow this way, that there were not enough hours in the day, and that the knowledge he passed on was being disseminated far too slowly and narrowly. He had retired to Ak'lehr, to the college where the church trained its elite. He had taken to writing and teaching, making sure that what he knew would still be available to the empire after his death. And he had brought up his family. He had tried to give them not only his knowledge, but also his purpose—the mission which had become obsessive in his own mind and which had been made sacred by the priests of Y'su. They had inherited it without any of the reservations that Bernhard Verheyden may have had. He had protected them from doubt with the fierceness of his indoctrination. He had protected them, too, from the sedition that had occasionally been preached by his companions, who had cooperated in his work in the interests of making a good living for themselves, but who had never quite believed in it. Jan said little about those other men, and I dared not press him too hard.

Rome was not build in a day, and neither was Ak'lehr. Papa Verheyden died with his revolution hardly begun. The seeds he had sown were beginning to bear fruit, but very slowly.

The metal-working industry had absorbed many of the lessons which he had to teach them, but their sights were not set as high as his—there was no way they could be. Production of iron and steel rose greatly, but the greater part of the metal went to the making of swords and tools and guns in great profusion. The priorities of the industry were largely set by the military, who were quick to see the advantage of cannon, but slow to appreciate the benefits of the steam engine. And so, though the seeds were planted, the industrial revolution remained an embryo. The priests played games with electricity, and made toys. But the time would come. It was only a matter of positive feedback . . . and once the loop was fully sealed, the growth would be exponential.

Verheyden had not been able to reproduce himself in his children. That was inevitable. Growing up in an alien culture they had inevitably become much more a part of that culture than their father could have. They had gone into various walks of life armed with all the advantages their father's knowledge could give them, but with limited vision. Only Piet and Anna had made the capital city their permanent home, and teaching their life's work. Jan had become a shipbuilder, Charles a builder of dams and canals, Christian an agronomist. These three younger brothers had lost a good deal of the sense of power which had obsessed their father and their elder brother. They were more modest in their ambitions, however strongly they still held on to the sense of mission that had been instilled into them. They believed in their father without really trying to emulate him. They had their own concerns and interests to look after, their own more limited lives.

All this I learned at second hand during the voyage up the coast of Delta in *Ilah'y'su*. It was an image seen through a murky glass—filtered through Jan's conversation with Mariel's aid. As we stopped at various ports I got glimpses of the empire, but we were never still for more than a couple of hours. Jan had business dealings to attend to, but he wasted not a second. He was in a hurry to get us back to Ak'lehr—to get us, in fact, off his hands. Being a younger brother has its privileges—one being that you can always pass the buck. Jan was determined that we weren't going to be his problem. He didn't know what our arrival really signified, and he was pleased—once I'd soothed his initial fears—to stop thinking about it. Piet could do the hard worrying and the decision-making.

I looked forward to meeting Piet with more than a little trepidation. I would have been interested to meet Bernhard Verheyden, because I had confidence that I would have been able to talk to him. We could have understood one another and the situation. We need not necessarily have been able to find any measure of agreement, and in the end Bernhard Verheyden might have come to see me as a threat to his plans that must be destroyed, but there would have been a certain common perspective. With Piet there was no such guarantee. I remembered James Wildeblood and the inheritors of *his* legacy of intrigue and control. The son could hardly have the mind of the father—he would be an echo of it, and so much more difficult to deal with because of it.

Comparing Verheyden and Wildeblood, I was disposed to meditate on the fact that such men were a natural product of the colony program. It is hardly surprising that the star-worlds should attract and produce empire-builders though Earth has seen none for centuries. All of Earth's empires are not only already built but already falling into ruins; every last one in the grip of terminal decay. Attica, like Wildeblood, still had virtually all of its history in front of it. Even the Ak'lehrian Empire was but recently emerged from prehistory. But on Wildeblood there had never been any doubt that the empire would be a human one. It would never come into bitter conflict with the Salamen because there was nothing to fight over. The land where the terrestrial forms of the aliens lived were of no use or interest to the human population. On Attica, things were different. When the colony had landed, it had seemed that a sensible balance could be easily achieved and maintained. The colony would take Lambda for its own, while the aliens would keep Delta. Not for three centuries would there even be the possibility of conflict.

Bernhard Verheyden had altered all that. He had tipped the balance of power and tipped it dramatically. There was a possibility that it could never be recovered.

15

Ak'lehr was crowded.

It was a city of contrasts. It had its fine stone buildings—its masterpieces of architecture whose shells would last for thousands of years as reminders to posterity of the achievements made by the Ore'l in the very cradle of their civilization. Had it consisted only of these stone terraces and palaces and neat square shops and dwelling places it would have been a well-planned, attractive city, open and pleasant. But it did not. Everywhere there was a vertical wall there were parasitic growths of wood and loose brick extending as high as mechanical possibility permitted. For every stone-walled shop there were a thousand street stalls. For every stone dwelling, neatly enclosed by its high wall, there were a thousand shanties and another thousand families without shelter of any kind. There were tents and lean-tos pitched in every blind alley, and in every street but the main thoroughfares (which were kept clear by the army) there was a constant battle to invade the space in the center—the no-man's-land where men and animals walked. There were people living in the streets in every state of abject poverty and despair.

People flock from rural areas into cities because that's the way that wealth flows. As a population explodes upon the land it must equalize by migration, and hope is where the city is. A city gathers a population as vast as it can contain. It attracts thieves and honest men alike, in such profusion that its beautiful buildings—the core which will become its echo and its memory in centuries to come—become a skeleton of respectability overgrown by a flesh of squalor. Inside the armored doors and the spiked gates there were neat gardens and pleasant houses. Outside, the poor divided up the pavements among themselves, distributing their excreta as convenience demanded. A maze of city walls enclosed two different worlds. Where men can only walk or ride there can be no suburban sprawl. Everything is piled together into one gigantic antheap.

The men of the city—I say "men" because the Ore'l were not so different as to make the term seem strange—presented a complete cross-section of cultural types. The poorest dressed in loincloths, with only their light fur to protect them against cold nights. There were many dressed like the sailors of *Ilah'y'su* in short skirts and jackets of various kinds. Some wore robes of various designs and color schemes, but the robes were invariably simple, like monkish habits rather than the classical togas of Earth. Curiously—or so it seemed to me—the priests of the city did not wear such robes, but light tunics of a very frail fabric which was often frayed or torn. Most carried satchels of some kind. The various ranks of the army were distinguished by insignia painted on the leathery jackets that they wore; the various ranks of the priesthood by decorations added to the hems and seams of the frail garments.

There are places on Earth now where similar cities still exist—civilizations stillborn because the resources of their various lands were long since plundered by better-established empires. But the Earthly antheap cities are cities without a future. Ak'lehr still had its future in hand and all its hopes were possibilities.

As we made our way through the streets from the docks eyes turned to watch us from everywhere. We had an armed escort of soldiers, who were armed with rifles instead of the crossbows which Jan's crew carried for "protection" against forest savages and dissident tradesmen. Rumors of our coming had flown ahead of us, though not too far. We were hot news. More messengers of god.

Or. . . .

No doubt, if circumstances seemed to warrant it, Piet and the leaders of the church could think of another way to account for us.

In one of the largest buildings in the very center of Ak'lehr—in an enclave that was virtually a city within a city, where the poor thronged the streets by day but were excluded by night—we were presented to the divine king,

Ir'is'hesh, son of Ir'ha'ra. The presentation was formal—a mere ritual. The king from his throne glanced down at us, to recognize our presence and to give us his provisional blessing. We did not approach within twenty meters. Once the formality was over we were whisked away, leaving the king to disappear into the House of Ir'ha'ra, returning to his godlike isolation. We were taken to another building, equally impressive and much more extensive than the palace—the temple of Y'su and the college that had grown around and behind it.

Here there was no ceremony. We were taken directly to Piet Verheyden. He received us in his own quarters. Anna and Christian were also there.

Piet was about thirty-three. He was tall, thin-framed, with the same light brown eyes and muddily fair hair as Jan. His voice was rather harsh, as though he had some minor injury or infection in his throat.

Anna was clearly stamped from the same mold. Though shorter she had the same kind of build and the same set to her features, but her eyes were hazel rather than brown. She wore her hair cut short, in the same style as Piet's, and this enhanced the resemblance considerably. Jan, in fact, looked the odd one of the three because his hair grew longer and his skin was tanned and coarse by comparison.

But Christian was something altogether different. He was short and sturdy, his features much more rounded. His eyes, his complexion and his hair were all much darker than those of his kindred. His oddness was accentuated by an old wound which had left a crescent-shaped scar around the line of the outer orbit of his right eye. There was no solid evidence, but the idea formed in my mind immediately that Christian was the child of a different father.

After the introductions we were offered food and drink, which we accepted gratefully. Life aboard the ship had been far too much like life aboard the *New Hope*, and the food only a little better. Now we enjoyed a meal meant not only to nourish but also to provide enjoyment. I noticed that Jan sat on our side of the table—it was as though he were being required to take some kind of responsibility for us. It was Jan who told most of our story to Piet and the others—Nieland and I interrupted occasionally to correct misleading impressions, or to confirm statements which Jan made, but we made few long speeches on our own account. Mariel, engaged in the business of scanning them minutely, said absolutely nothing. It was not until the meal was completely finished that any real dialogue began.

"I must apologize for Charles' absence," said Piet. "I'm afraid that I don't know when he'll return. He is supervising the building of a dam in the far southwest. Reports suggest that it isn't going well. There's a panic throughout that region because of an epidemic of some kind. We're even having trouble keeping the roads open."

"It might be as well to keep the roads closed," I observed. "It's roads that spread diseases."

Piet laughed. It was the laugh of an experienced man of the world when he hears something naively amusing. "There are always diseases in the south. It's largely a matter of hygiene. The towns along the roads have little to fear."

"From what I've seen of the city," I said, "hygiene is a big problem even here."

Piet frowned. "We have excellent hospitals," he said. "Our influence here has advanced medical practice from stupid superstition to standards which are extremely high. It's true that the sewage system can't cope with the problem at present, but it's only a matter of a few years and tighter controls on the scavengers that flock through our gates. I assure you that we can cope. Our domestic medical problems are being defeated, slowly but surely. As for sickness out of the southern swamps . . . they're hot climate diseases. They only thrive in the outlying districts.

"In any case, all this is beside the point. I'd rather discuss your plans. You came here to study the Ore'l?"

"To make contact," I affirmed. "Or, since contact has already been made, to study the results of the association. We must report back to Earth on the state of affairs that exists on both Lambda and Delta."

"For what reason?"

"Reason?" I parried.

"Why does Earth want to know what is happening here? Didn't you abandon us more than a hundred years ago?"

"There has been a long gap between contacts," I admitted. "But Earth did not 'abandon' any of the colonies. That was never the UN's intention. It was a matter of supplying the necessary help at the correct times. Time had to elapse for the problems of each individual colony to materialize, for the specific kinds of aid required to become clear."

"And what kind of aid did you bring?" he asked.

"A laboratory equipped for ecological analysis and for the genetic modification of both species originally brought from Earth and those native to Attica."

"Genetic modification of the *colonists*?" said Christian, incredulously.

"Hardly," I replied. "That's too complex—not to mention illegal. Modification of plants . . . the development of strains resistant to various forms of parasitic attack. The only organisms we can actually *build* are viruses . . . though we can build single genes or groups of genes to produce specific proteins into most lower animals and plants. Engineering people is a problem of an entirely different order. Basically we eradicate pests and help crops negotiate metabolic bottlenecks. It's a subtle form of ecological management, but we're often represented to the vulgar viewpoint as ratcatchers. With our help, the colony should be able to overcome all the difficulties that have hit its food supply."

"And you think that you arrived at the right moment?" said Piet.

"No," I said. "We might have done more had we arrived earlier. But we did not realize, on Earth, that the colonies would be so badly crippled by the difficulties of co-adaptation. The UN made a mistake in the general pattern of its thinking."

"A hundred years," said Piet, sarcastically. "A little mistake of a few decades, a few generations."

"Earth has problems too," I said. "Problems which are much more difficult to solve. We may have underestimated yours . . . but we've never been able to underestimate our own. Yes, help should have come sooner. You have a right to be bitter. But all the colonies had to take their place on a scale of priorities. Men suffered in the colony here for lack of support . . . but they also suffered on Earth. They still are suffering. And they're bitter, too. They're bitter now because help *is* being sent out to the colonies, just as the colonists have been bitter because such resources as there were fifty years ago were being used on Earth. And the Lambda colony has survived. Some didn't."

"The Lambda colony was determined to survive," said Piet, with a sneer in his voice. "So determined that it very nearly didn't. It drove out the one man who could have saved it. If things had been different perhaps it wouldn't have needed *your* help at all."

The element of doublethink in Piet's logic was clear. He was bitter because Earth hadn't sent aid to Attica earlier. He was also bitter because the colony had ungraciously rejected his father, who would have brought it through its time of trouble without need of aid from Earth. But human minds can accommodate much more contradictory ideas with ease. There was nothing remarkable about it.

"It appears to me," I said, trying to sound anything *but* sarcastic, "that *you*'re in an ideal position now to offer aid to the colony. You've done a great deal here to help the Ore'l . . . you'll go down in history as their benefactors. You could write yourself a place in colony history, too . . . as the people who secured the future of two continents."

I hadn't really intended to put the cat among the pigeons quite so soon. But Piet had seemed bent on cutting right to the heart of the matter and he had dragged me right along with him.

"You think the colony would hail us as heroes?" he said. "They'd curse us as they cursed our father."

"How do you know?"

He laughed. Again it was the laugh of the worldly wise confronted with the naive. But he didn't answer the question. Instead, he said: "This is our home. The Ore'l are our people. Our father turned his back on the colony as it turned its back on him. The colony's troubles are no concern of ours. We have our own work to do."

He struck me as being a master of unsubtlety. With a little practice he could have doubled for a comic-opera villain. But I had to remember that he was part feral child. He had known only a handful of human beings in all his life—most of them his immediate family. He had never had to learn generalized techniques and responses for dealing with others of his own kind—only for dealing with the aliens, whom he placed in a very different existential category. I knew that it was going to be difficult to talk to him. His mind didn't have much capacity for flexibility. Even less than Jan's. The idea of contact with Lambda would make sense to Jan, in the context of trade. But to Piet, it simply sounded like heresy against what he'd been taught to believe. He had no means of access to the idea—it was closed around by walls that Bernhard Verheyden had built.

I looked at the others. I couldn't begin to fathom what they were thinking, but I knew that Mariel would tell me later. No one of them seemed to manifest the open hostility that was in Piet's eyes and voice. Jan, over the period of the voyage, had grown accustomed to us, and felt a certain responsibility for us simply because he had brought us here. Anna watched me closely, but seemed interested in what I had to say. Christian didn't watch me at all. He seemed to have other things on his mind.

A long silence developed while I waited. The general atmosphere was uncomfortable. I guessed that there were some tensions here that had nothing to do with us. Old disagreements, temporarily submerged while we were here but not forgotten. Perhaps something to do with the epidemic in the distant provinces. Perhaps something much deeper than any issues of state.

"You're mistaken about the attitude of the colony's government," said Nieland, in the tone of a man who feels duty-bound to speak but doesn't know how to say what it is he intends to convey. "We would welcome trade with Delta. It could be of great value to both of us. When the *Floreat* set sail, you know, that was partly its purpose

. . . to establish contact with the aliens and to explore the possibilities of trade. It was part of your father's mission."

"You know something about our father's mission," said Piet, his voice like a knife edge.

"But don't you see?" Nieland continued. "The colony will build more ships now. Once it's known that you're here . . . the colony will *want* to trade. You can't keep Ak'lehr to yourself forever, you know. . . ."

He let go the end of the sentence unhappily, knowing he'd gone too far. It was with difficulty that I refrained from raising my eyes to heaven in despair. He had really laid the issue open, now. There wasn't a mind in the room that couldn't run on to all the *ifs* that were stacked inside Nieland's statement. Including the most important *if* of all: *if* Piet Verheyden let us go back to Lambda.

The tension was redoubled while Piet stared at Nieland and let the thoughts pass slowly across his mind, unaware that Mariel was reading their every nuance.

Then there was a knock on the door.

It opened to admit an alien in the flimsy garments of a priest. I hadn't yet learned the meaning of the various insignia, but I guessed from his youth that he was a novice. He spoke to Piet in his own language.

If Piet's expression had been dark before, it now grew positively thunderous. He spat back half a dozen words in Ak'lehrian. The youth in the doorway quailed somewhat, but answered at some length. Piet suppressed his anger and gave an equally lengthy answer. The youth left.

I glanced at Mariel, hoping that she had managed to glean some significance from the exchange. She nodded slightly. I looked at Piet.

"Ul'el would like to see you," he said. "It is, I fear, unavoidable. I told him that you were very tired because of your journey and could not see him tonight. I said that all three of you could be formally presented to the officers of church and college in the morning. It's not what he wanted, but it's what he'll get." He glanced briefly at Jan.

"I told them nothing," said Jan. "I thought it best to leave such matters to you."

Piet looked pleased, for the first time.

"Ul'el," he said to me, "is one of the magisters of the

church. I don't know quite how to render his title into English, but magister is what my father called him. We refer to the others either by that name, or as officers, or as masters, but Ul'el is always a magister. You will understand that our presence here is not equally appreciated by everyone. There are those who are jealous of the influence we have, of the things we have done for the empire. Insofar as the opposition is organized at all, it is organized around Ul'el. He is our enemy, if that is not too strong a word. Christian will probably say that it is, but I think it is a correct assessment."

Christian made no objection to this comment, but simply looked elsewhere while Piet's eyes rested on him.

"Be careful of Ul'el," said Piet, quietly. "He is your enemy too. He is sure to use your coming here against us, in some way. Don't talk to him unless one of us—Anna or myself—is with you."

I was interested by the way that "one of us" translated into "Anna or myself." I was also interested in Ul'el.

"In what way does he oppose you?" I asked.

"He is jealous of our influence," said Piet, simply repeating the formula he had used previously.

I let it go. "Well," I said. "You were right in what you told our visitor. We *are* tired after our long journey. Very tired. We'd like to retire to our rooms now."

He looked slightly surprised by this, and almost raised an objection. But they were his own words that we were quoting back at him, and though they'd been the most obvious of pretexts he didn't want to deny them.

And so the party—not the best one I'd ever been to— broke up.

16

Our apartments were quite handsome. They were, in fact, quite the best accommodation I'd had since leaving Earth—and, on reflection, a good deal better than anything I'd ever enjoyed *on* Earth. They had central heating, private bathrooms, and good furniture. They were less spacious than Piet's, but otherwise similar. We all had three rooms each. There were no connecting doors, but we were all on the same corridor.

I wasted no time in seeking out Mariel as soon as I was rid of Anna, who had been appointed to show me where everything was.

She was testing the softness of the bed, and apparently finding it to her liking.

"Too soft," I said. "Give you a backache."

I sat down in a chair. All Ak'lehrian chairs had high backs. Most of them also had long legs, but the ones in our rooms had been specially shortened for humans.

"Heavy," she said. She wasn't talking about the bed.

"All right," I said. "Let's start with Piet."

"He's mad," she observed.

"We already knew that. What's his immediate reaction to us?"

"He's scared," she replied. "Our arrival here is an unlooked-for complication in a situation that's already tense, for a great many reasons I can't begin to guess. He's worried about this epidemic, he's worried about his brothers—all three of them—and he's worried about this priest-character. Those worries I could see . . . there are probably more. He wants to keep us in his pocket. He has vague ideas about being able to use us, provided that we're obliging puppets. He has no intention of shipping us back to Lambda—not at present. Maybe not ever. He wants to spend a good long time finding out what we've come here for and what kind of force is at the back of us.

He's paranoid . . . but we knew that already. He's *very* paranoid."

"What's he got against his brothers?" I asked.

She shrugged. "Can't tell exactly. He and Christian are bristling with mutual hostility. He mistrusts Jan, although Jan doesn't seem aware of it. Possibly it's nothing specific . . . just a manifestation of the paranoia. He seems to have a curiously intense reaction when he refers to Anna. Maybe he feels she's the only one he can trust. Maybe it's more than that."

"Brotherly love," I said. She didn't reply, but left me to draw my own conclusions.

"What do the others think of us?" I asked.

"Christian seems quite pleased to see us," she said. "He's not hostile. But that mighty simply be a reflection of the fact that Piet *is*. Any enemy of yours is a friend of mine and all that. Anna. . . ."

There was a pause.

"Well?" I asked.

"Anna's feelings are mixed," she said. "I wouldn't like to attempt a summation. She's confused. But basically, she's with Piet."

She didn't seem disposed to go into more detail. I pressed on: "What about that conversation with the alien?" I asked.

"What was said was probably what Piet reported," she told me. "I'm slowly getting the hang of the language, thanks to Al'ha and one or two of the others aboard ship. Reading between the lines is still beyond me. But the situation really brought out Piet's paranoia—as you presumably saw. At first he wanted to tell Ul'el to go to hell, but he had to modify it because of the way the alien framed the request. What he offered was a compromise . . . and an empty one. We'd have to be introduced to the powers-that-be anyhow. Piet wants to keep us very much his property—to meditate between the aliens and us. He seems pretty confident in that department. After all, he knows everything and we're outsiders who know nothing. He thinks he can work us like puppets. If he knew about my talents, maybe he wouldn't be so sure."

"No," I said. "Maybe he wouldn't."

There was a pause.

"Nieland's scared," she said, pulling the observation out of the vacuous silence.

"I noticed," I replied. "He's out of his depth. He's a shipbuilder at heart. The only one he has anything in common with is Jan. But he's still our link. We need him if we can talk them round."

"They'll never accept him as a kindred spirit to their father," she stated flatly.

I'd already come to that conclusion.

"You'll have to talk to him," I said. "You can read him. You'll know how to guide him. You've got to get him into some kind of shape to be the colony's ambassador to Ak'lehr. Like it or not, that's what he is."

"I'll try," she promised.

"And in the meantime . . ." I mused.

She caught something in the tone of my voice and looked hard at my eyes.

"If you're planning what I think you're planning. . . ."

"Why the if?" I asked. "Losing your touch?"

"It's a bit precipitate," she said. "We've only been here a matter of hours. Couldn't you just play it cool for a few days. We aren't going to be murdered in our beds. We've plenty of time."

"I'm not going to be used as a pawn in a chess game," I said. "It's an existential situation that I don't find too comfortable. And that's the way Piet's going to play it. He already is. I don't know what he's doing, but I know he's under pressure. I think the best thing to do is to establish myself as a player instead of a piece. That way I'm less likely to end up being moved to a square I don't want to occupy."

"He's not going to like it," she said. "Annoying paranoids isn't diplomatic. Plotting against them is downright dangerous. It confirms all their nastiest feelings."

"He doesn't have to know," I said. "I'll wait until all good humans should be in their beds."

"Don't be a fool," she said, unkindly. "How can you stop him finding out?"

I just looked at her levelly, and let her read the rest.

She saw that I was determined simply in the fact of my silence.

"Be careful," she advised.

"Look after yourself," I answered. "I need you. You're our secret weapon, remember."

"I know," she said, not without bitterness. "I know."

17

It is said that life imitates art. It's probably true—most people wouldn't know how to go about the business of living if they didn't have *something* to imitate. One might, however, make the corollary observation that life has very bad taste.

In virtually every melodrama featuring primitive societies written while such romances were in their heyday there is a villain, and he is always the high priest. He is either small and thin and bald with glittering eyes and an evil disposition or tall and thin and bald with glittering eyes and an evil disposition. He resents the respect in which his hitherto docile flock hold the noble and humane heroes who have come from the world outside and are putting a stop to his human sacrifices and general terrorist activities. He is a phantasm invented by Christians and adopted by rationalists to symbolze the evils of paganism and superstition.

The power which such stereotypes have over the human imagination is absurd but alarming. These ruts in our minds might be hacked out crudely with stone-age chisels, but they are nonetheless effective when it comes to channeling thought. It seems that there is something basic within us that responds to such ludicrous caricatures and their characteristically overwritten menace. No matter how wise we become we always have to fight to crush the tissue of our nightmares.

Trepidation would be too casual a word to describe what I felt as I knocked gently upon the door and opened it. My heart was hammering with an irrational fear . . . a fear far more dangerous *because* it was irrational. A great deal might hinge upon this meeting, and the presence of that evil, stupid phantasm could so easily spoil it.

Ul'el, despite the lateness of the hour, was still awake. He was seated before his desk, with papers everywhere—

scattering the desk-top, piled upon the floor, heaped on shelves behind him. Most of them were loosely bound into great sheaves, wrapped around with protective covers of soft leather.

He looked up as I entered. I was learning to read alien faces, but there are some emotions whose reflections appear so rarely that one hardly has a chance to master them. I could not tell whether he was astonished or so calm that he showed no surprise. He made a sudden, brisk series of gestures, tidying up the mess on his desk somewhat. He nodded toward a chair. I had to drag it a few meters across the room, and must have appeared rather clumsy in so doing. When I sat down my feet did not touch the floor—this chair had not been specially re-molded for human use.

"I believe you wanted to see me," I said.

He looked at me, carefully and unhurriedly. Because he was seated I couldn't tell how tall he was, but he seemed like a person of considerable size. His fur was paler than was usual among his kind—a tawny yellow, with reddish marks. His eyes didn't glitter unduly, though they did seem a little bright because the only illumination in the room was the electric desk lamp he had been using for study.

"I know it's late," I said, trying to keep my voice level and show no sign of embarrassment, "but I felt it best to be discreet."

"How did you find me?" he asked. Like Al'ha he had difficulty in pronouncing certain consonants, but he did not substitute the indeterminate throatal pauses common in his own speech. He tried very hard to work within his natural limitations, and with a fair degree of success. I had no difficulty understanding him.

"I slipped away from our corner of the building and just walked until I found one of your people. He didn't speak English but all I had to do was keep repeating your name. He wouldn't hang about, though—he just showed me the door and beat a hasty retreat."

He made a small sound in his throat, as though clearing it. "You are the man from Earth," he said.

"Alexis Alexander," I agreed.

"I am Ul'el," he said, just to make it clear. "Why did you come?"

"I wanted to talk to you," I told him. "Piet Verheyden isn't an easy man to deal with. He regards us as his personal property. We're not. We didn't come here to see him, or to deal with him. Our business is with people who are empowered to speak for Ak'lehr."

He was still studying me minutely. He didn't trust me. How could he?

"The children have told you about me?" he asked.

"I think you know what they have told me," I replied.

"They are children," he said. "Only children. They are trying hard to hold on to what they were. I knew their father well. I was one of his pupils, though I was adult when Piet was a small boy. I learned his language and his writing. He taught me everything . . . freely. He taught me because he wanted me to know. He did not make conditions. The children . . . they do not see that what is freely given is freely to be used. They bargain. They think that they have a right to administer what they have learned with us, as though it were somehow their own. They have turned themselves against us. They have made us into enemies by attempting to make demands which were never theirs to make. They are still trying to exercise a proprietary right over what is free, what is now *ours*. Do you see what I mean?"

"Yes," I said.

"They have told you that I am plotting against them . . . that I want to undermine their authority . . . that I am jealous of their influence. All of these things are true. You must understand this, if we are to talk. Had you not come here as you did, I would have held this back, let it remain covert, at least for a while. But you have come to talk, and it is well that we are honest. I do not consider that we owe the children anything. They think that all that their father gave us somehow remains theirs. But they learned it alongside us. Everything they know came from the same source, in the same way, as what Bernhard Verheyden taught me and a hundred others. Even to their father we owe no debts. We are grateful for what we now have, but it was *sika'y'su,* a gift from god. It does not

112

matter whether you understand this as metaphor or literal truth."

"I understand," I said. "How is it that the children still have any influence at all?"

He performed a strange gesture, touching his fingertips to his forehead and then raising his hand slightly into the air.

"Ilah'y'su," he said.

"Messengers of god?" I couldn't quite see what he was getting at.

"They partake of the divine spark," he said, and I was sure that he chose the words in order to indicate irony. "I have been talking in essentially secular terms. But I am a man of god. We owe nothing . . . but there is a sense in which we hold the children . . . valuable? The word does not fit. But in your language it is not quite possible to convey the meaning. A difference in the way of thinking."

I pondered for a few moments, trying to sort things out.

"You don't want them here," I said. "They're not useful to you. You don't feel that you owe them anything, on a straightforward commercial level, speaking in secular terms. They're trying to interfere with the way in which you apply and control the knowledge that Bernhard Verheyden gave you, and you don't think that they have the right to do it—or even that *he* had the right to do it. But you won't move against them openly. You won't imprison them or murder them or even compel them to leave. For reasons deriving from your religious ethics."

"That seems to be a fair summary," agreed Ul'el.

"You're tied in a knot of your own making," I observed.

"Y'su made the knot," he corrected me, gently. "And if human people were caught in a similar situation? Would they not recognize the force of moral dilemmas? Would they not find a gap between what is right and what is convenient? Would they not hesitate?"

"I think so," I replied. "Ninety-nine men in a hundred would hesitate. We find such knots in our day-to-day lives. There are always men who cut them with swords, but for the most part. . . ."

"We have such men too," said Ul'el, quietly.

"Yes," I said, remembering a battle in a tiny forest village, and a tall fighting man armed with a steel blade striking down a woman who was running for shelter. I remembered the burning of homes, and of flesh, and the explanation that they were *only forest savages*.

"It is important that you understand all this," said Ul'el. "If you can."

"The reason you wanted to see me," I said, carefully, "was to check me out. Either me, or Nieland. What you want from us, ultimately, is that we should take the children off your back . . . take them back to the colony. You want to know whether we're in sympathy with that aim."

"If such a thing were possible," said Ul'el, as though meditating aloud. "If the ilah'y'su were to decide that their mission was complete. If they were to bid us a fond farewell, and sail away, in the ship named *Ilah'y'su*. . . . we would be grieved to see them go. But in a way, we might also be happy. It is not easy to be in the presence of the divine king . . . it is a delicate business, the day-by-day negotiation with the incarnation of Y'su. When it is complicated. . . .

"The knot is not so easily untangled, if you see what I mean."

"No," I answered, "the knot is not so easily untangled. If we were in a position to persuade the Verheydens to return to the colony it might be a little easier . . . but there are knots and knots. We're in no position to compel them to give up what they think they have here. To be quite honest, I'd be glad to persuade them to give up their sense of mission, because I think that it's dangerous. But to suppose that the whole situation could be healed by their sailing away . . . no, that won't do."

Ul'el said nothing in reply. He waited for me to go on.

"How do you see the future?" I asked him. "I mean, what kind of future do you envisage for your people, and for this world as a whole?"

"I'm not a fortune-teller," he answered.

"You know I'm not asking you for a set of predictions," I replied, quietly. "You must know what I'm talking about. I'm talking about Armageddon, if the word means anything to you. Ak'lehr is extending its dominion by conquest. Your armies are marching, and with them your priests. Your ambitions as a race—the ambitions of your god—are very practical ones. Not for you the welfare of the spirit and the afterlife. Y'su's rewards, like his kings and his messengers, are to be effective here, in the real world.

"You'll conquer all of Delta. There isn't anything that can stop you. But what then? When empires extend to their limits there's no future for them but internal division, conflict, fragmentation. When the time comes, will you accept that? Will you fight against the internal strife and try to build Utopia . . . or will you take the easier course, the more natural course? Will you attempt to extend your dominion still farther . . . across the ocean?"

"No one can predict the future," said Ul'el. "It is in the hands of Y'su."

"It's in our hands," I contradicted him. "Not necessarily yours and mine . . . though perhaps even that . . . but in the hands of our respective peoples. We make the future out of the substance of the present. Our children . . . and what we give to them . . . *are* the future. Y'su may be in charge of it all, somewhere and somehow, but we're the people here—we're the ones who'll perform the actions that will create the world to come."

"That is vanity," said Ul'el. "Vanity is deadly."

"It's not vanity," I declared stubbornly. "It's not even pride. It's not a matter of blasphemously robbing Y'su of his prerogatives. It's a matter of accepting the responsibility for our own actions. In the sight of Y'su, or any other god, we must be prepared to decide between good and evil . . . not just the good and evil of the moment, but all the good and evil yet to come. It is not vanity to try to recognize the consequences of our actions today, tomorrow and forever. It is our duty. We may try and fail, but if we do not even try . . . could you really look your god in the face and say: 'I took my decisions for the moment. I did not think about the future. I did not even try.'?"

You can't debate theology with an alien. There's no way you can make sense. You can't even debate theology with another human. It's a subject that doesn't acknowledge the concept of debate. If I made an impression on Ul'el it would have to be in the area of his secular thinking. I had to appeal to his political *persona,* and risk its getting tangled by his untranslatable relationship with his deity.

"I'll tell you how I see the future," I said. "On Attica's two continents will grow two nations. They will have little in common . . . not even a way of thinking or a biological heritage. Even leaving aside the fact that the humans came here from another planet, these two races live in different worlds—continents whose life-systems have evolved separately since their first emergence from the sea. Those two nations, if they insist that their first priorities are purely internal, concerned with their own affairs, their own land, their own wealth, will grow separately, each knowing that the other exists but hardly caring. At some time in the future—not the distant future, in historical terms, but only a few centuries—internal pressures will cause one or other of them to redirect its attentions outward. I don't know whether the trigger will be population pressure or greed, or simply the need to soothe internal conflicts by creating common enemies, but there will be a trigger and it will be pressed. Between these two nations there will be war. It will be a war that neither side can win, although temporary victories might be achieved. It will be a war that will go on forever and ever, that will never end even if it can be resolved. There are several possible resolutions, but one of them is this: if Earth should find out that one of its colonies is at war, then it will intervene, no matter what the cost. It will not intervene on the side of the humans, but as an independent power committed to restoring peace. Effectively, UN forces will conquer *both* nations. Both will lose, and become subject to an external power that will be just as alien to the colonists as to you.

"Perhaps you will consider that in all this, right is on your side. Perhaps you will consider that this is your world, that the humans should never have come, and that it is your sacred right to fight until they are forced to depart forever . . . or to kill you all. I don't know. I do

116

know that a lot of humans would agree with you. But the knot is tied. The situation is as it is. It matters little who tied the knot and whether they were right to do so.

"As I see the future, there is only one way to avoid this war, and that is to establish peace. I don't know whether this is possible. Maybe the future is determined—maybe Y'su has it all written down in his book and there's no way a feeble human or Ore'l mind can change a single word. But if we were to try, what we'd have to do is to bring the two nations together now, to establish links between them, to allow them to get to know one another, to help them to help one another. Bernhard Verheyden may have made a good start, although his motives weren't quite the motives I'd have chosen for him. If the children have their way, that start could be thrown away by the determination to hate the colony, to compete with it, to demonstrate to it how wrong it was to thwart their father's ambitions. But if you have your way, things will be no better. You want to get the children out of the way, so that you can get on with your own affairs your own way, using your precious gifts from god but acknowledging no debts in respect thereof.

"Humans tend to think of peace as a passive state—the absence of war. I don't know whether you think the same way. But peace can't be perpetuated passively. It has to be constructed. It has to be built and maintained, actively. Starting here. Starting now."

"There is a possibility," said Ul'el, in a strangely remote tone, "that you are ilah'y'su."

That may have been a little test. Either way, I wasn't having any.

"No, I'm not," I said. "I'm anything but that. I'm no messenger at all. I'm not trying to give orders or make requests. I'm telling you how I see the situation. It's not a god's eye view—nothing like it. This isn't about Y'su at all. It's about *us*, and what kind of decision *we* make, and what . . . in the end . . . comes of it."

I had come to Ul'el with a list of questions—some trivial, some whose importance I couldn't weigh up. He had short-circuited them all by making me put my whole case so soon and so directly. But all in all it seemed that we had cleared the air. He had wanted to see me, and he had told me why. I had wanted to see him, and I had told him why. There would be other meetings. We both had one hell of a lot to think about.

As I left, my legs still felt weak, and my throat still felt dry. The phantasm of the evil high priest was still haunting the corridors of my mind. There was no way to know whether I could trust Ul'el, or even whether I could say anything to him that would make sense in terms of his ways of thinking.

I returned to my own room in a kind of hypnotic daze, feeling absolutely exhausted.

18

I opened my door and went straight on into the darkness. I knew there was a light switch somewhere, but I couldn't be bothered groping for it. On a small table beside the bed was the lantern that had once been the property of a tribe of forest savages. By the light that came through the open door from the corridor I could see it.

After switching it on I turned to go back and shut the door, but I was brought up short by the realization that I was not alone. Sitting in the chair, concealed by its high back from the door and the light filtering through it from the corridor, was Piet Verheyden.

His jaw was tight. The expression in his eyes would probably have nauseated Mariel if she'd been required to read what was behind it.

Paranoids, I remembered, often didn't sleep too well. They are, as a matter of habit, night birds.

"Where have you been?" he said, in a laryngeal acid whisper.

"Out," I said, flatly.

It was a mistake. If I'd spoken smoothly and lightly, and answered at some length, I could have set the tone for the conversation. We could have spent the next half hour swapping sarcasms in honeyed tones. But the harshness of my clipped answer constituted a challenge.

"You've come here to destroy us," he said, still in that idiotic whisper. "You think you can take it all away from us. Well, you can't. It's *ours*. We built it . . . my father and I. No one will take it from us. Not you. Not Ul'el."

I didn't know what to say. I could hardly humor him, and I certainly didn't want to start a long and fierce argument.

"I'm tired," I said, finally. "I want to go to bed."

"Then why are you wandering the corridors at this time? You've been with Ul'el."

Whether it was a guess or whether he knew there was no way to tell. It didn't matter much.

"I did meet him," I agreed. "He explained his position. I explained mine. If it will reassure you, we didn't reach any measure of agreement. There is something of a gap between our aims. Is that what you wanted to know?"

He stared at me balefully.

"You don't realize the situation here," he said. "You're a stranger. You must allow us to be your guides. You must take my advice on all matters. We understand the situation. You do not. If you act unwisely. . . ."

The threat was naked in his words.

"I'll take my chances," I said. Again, the wrong thing—I was tired and my nerves were set on edge.

"And the girl?" he said. "You don't realize just how vulnerable you are here. You must let those who understand what is best be your guides and your protectors. Trafficking with Ul'el will bring nothing but trouble."

I wanted to tell him to get out, but I kept that much of my temper in hand.

Instead, I walked over to his chair and leaned close, supporting myself with a hand on the back.

"Why are you so scared?" I asked, in a low voice. "What's thrown you into this panic? Not just the general state of affairs, that's for sure. I meant to ask Ul'el, but I never quite got around to it. Why does this epidemic in the south frighten you so much?"

His face was livid with anger. I'd taken the initiative and was pressuring him. It's an easy thing to do when you're dealing with a paranoid . . . but it's not always a wise thing.

"The plague is nothing," he whispered. "It may kill a thousand peasants or a hundred thousand. Herdsmen and dirt farmers. But what they're saying—in the gutters of Ak'lehr as well as in the south—is that it's a judgment from god . . . from their beloved Y'su. They say that my father was a false messenger, a tempter, and that the plague is Y'su's punishment because the people listened. The rumor was deliberately started as a political attack upon the family. It's an attempt to discredit and dispossess us. It was started by Ul'el."

I stepped back, letting the force of his oration bleed some of the tension out of the situation.

"You're wrong," I said, after barely a moment to think it out. "However much Ul'el wants to discredit you, he doesn't want to discredit your father and the knowledge he brought to Ak'lehr—and he certainly doesn't want to discredit himself and the church for having listened to your father. Rumors like that come up from the bottom, they aren't started on top. It's an expression of resentment against the entire political hierarchy . . . if it had any real power it would be the banner of a revolution. But I don't believe it has."

He didn't take a lot of notice of my objections. That wasn't the way he saw it—he took it too personally for that. If anything, my little speech only confirmed his determined opinion that I couldn't understand what was at stake or what was going on here.

He got up from the chair. "I can handle this," he said. "I've handled it before. We've always been able to handle Ul'el and his kind. Just remember that I'm in control. I can crush you if I need to. Remember that, too."

"I will," I promised, making way for him as he went to the door. "I will."

He closed the door behind him, very quietly. I couldn't hear the sound of his footfalls as he went away down the passage.

I sat down on the bed and pulled off my boots, cursing silently. If Piet had achieved nothing else he had certainly revitalized my sense of our vulnerability here in Ak'lehr. For a while, talking to Ul'el, I had almost reached the illusory sense of being in control, of feeling things yield to my presence and my will. Now, that was gone, and I knew once more how helpless I really was.

Vanity, Ul'el had called my attempt to interfere here—to interfere with nothing less than the course of history. I had denied it. But vanity it was. A vain pursuit, in more than one sense of the word.

I got into bed, and went very rapidly to sleep.

I didn't get a backache.

19

I very nearly slept until noon. There was very little noise in the building or outside the window (which looked out on to an inner courtyard) and there was little to disturb my peace and luxury. I could have slept on and on, but I was interrupted by polite knocking at the door.

It was Mariel, already up and about. She seemed to disapprove of my situation. She had, of course, gone to bed rather earlier than I had.

"What is it?" I asked.

"Action," she replied. "Thought you'd like to know. Charles turned up. Family quarrel brewing."

I sat up, rubbing my eyes and trying to clear my head.

"What sort of quarrel?"

"Charles had trouble getting into the city. Rumor apparently had it that he'd brought the plague back with him. What he seems to have brought is some animals and a few sick men. They're still outside the walls. Piet is pretty mad."

I could guess why. If he was worried about rumors concerning the epidemic being a personal statement by Y'su he was going to construe Charles' action in bringing it to the gates of Ak'lehr as a monumental stroke of stupidity.

I eased myself from the bed and dressed quickly.

"Where are they?" I asked.

"Piet's rooms," she replied.

I reflected sadly that it was a pity to have missed breakfast, but followed her along the corridor and up the staircase. The row was still going strong when we got here. Piet was pacing up and down, almost trembling with anger. The others stood still in various corners of the room. Anna was well back, with the table in between herself and the others, taking little or no part. The one that I hadn't seen before—Charles—was standing about a meter

122

inside the doorway, with Christian by his side. Both were stationed at right angles to the path of Piet's prowling line. Jan was away to the side, participating but not overtly taking one side or the other. Mariel and I slipped in behind the co-defendants and moved to a station opposite Jan's. Only Anna glanced at us for more than a fraction of a second.

"I think he's right!" Christian was saying.

"You *would* think he's right," rasped Piet, with some vituperation.

"You could at least listen," suggested Charles. The second of the four brothers was physically the most impressive—he was slightly taller than Piet but much more solidly built. His resemblance to Piet and Jan might otherwise have been clear had he not sported a beard that concealed much of the lower part of his face in a tangle of pale brown curly hair.

"Piet," put in Jan, "there's no point in this. It's done now. Why rave about it? We're committed. Let's get on with it."

"*It's done now!*" mimicked Piet, throwing up his hands in a histrionic gesture. "I hear nothing else. All of you . . . you just carry on without thinking . . . you foul things up right, left and center. And you come to me and say 'Never mind what I ought to have done. Never mind what I ought to have thought. It's done now.' And you expect *me* to. . . ."

"Nobody expects *you* to do anything," Charles cut in.

"You make me *sick!*" said Piet. "The lot of you. You bring the plague to our very doorstep and Jan brings. . . ."

He had stopped and half-turned to point at us. He had known that we were in the room, but it had not quite impinged upon his consciousness until he'd actually referred to us. Now he thought to question our presence. He checked the pointing finger and dropped his arm.

"What are you doing here?" he asked.

"Is there anything I can do to help?" I asked, pleasantly.

There was a chorus of contradictory answers. Christian and Jan both said "Yes," and all but drowned out Piet's

"No." The mixed reaction surprised me, but it seemed to reinfuriate Piet. He didn't know quite which one of his brothers to attack. Jan stepped quickly forward to take hold of his arm.

"Listen, Piet," he said. "There's no point in all this. Perhaps Charles acted precipitately. But he had his reasons, and there's some merit in them. If we *can* do as he says then we can destroy this stupid rumor just like *that*. And Alex can help. If there's one man who *can* do it, it's Alex. And don't you see what that will do for us? An emergency arises, and in the very moment that panic begins to spread new human visitors arrive . . . and through them we cope with the emergency. *Ilah'y'su*! Who could deny it?"

While Jan was speaking I began to have small doubts about the role that he was carving out for me, but it didn't seem to be the right moment to object. If this was a chance to get a foot in the door. . . .

But Piet was already answering. "Oh yes!" he said, his voice almost a hiss. "And what then? He takes our place, I suppose. He becomes the successor to our father. And what do we do? Go to the sea, like you? Become dambuilders, like idiot Charles? What are you trying to *do* to us?"

"Don't be a fool," said Christian. "The Ore'l aren't going to discriminate between us. As far as they're concerned we're all humans, all one family. Whatever he does can only work in favor of all of us. He doesn't want to take our place, or take up where our father left off. Do you?"

The last question was addressed to me.

"No," I answered, truthfully.

Piet, still seething with fury, looked around for support. Jan had definitely taken his stance alongside Charles and Christian. Anna was still standing well back. When he looked at her she gave no sign of support, and said nothing.

"You'll destroy us all!" he said, his voice still twisted by the infection in his throat—if infection it was. He was facing Charles as he said it, but the condemnation was meant much more generally. He turned away, then, and walked to the inner door of the suite, which presumably led through to the bedroom. He closed it behind him with a crash.

"We'd better go to my room," said Christian, He moved toward the door. We all moved with him except Anna. Jan turned as we left, and said to her: "Are you coming?"

She shook her head slowly. Jan shrugged.

Christian's room was only a few doors down the corridor. We all went inside. He indicated soundlessly that we should sit down. There were only two armchairs—Jan took one and Mariel the other. The rest of us took chairs from the table and moved them around so that we could all see one another. The atmosphere was tense. Christian still seemed angry about the quarrel and embarrassed about his anger. Jan, too, was angry—perhaps because Piet had referred unkindly to his own action in bringing us to Ak'lehr. Charles just looked deflated by the whole thing.

Jan introduced us to the newcomer, with mock formality.

"What makes you think I can help?" I asked, already having more than a suspicion.

"Charles had better tell it," said Christian. "From the beginning."

Charles gathered himself together a little. "We've been building a dam on a river in the far southwest," he said. "We occupy the territory—which is to say, we lay claim to it all and have established army posts in most of the major settlements. We've pushed the road through. There's lots of good land there, once the trees are cleared from the hills, and there could be a great deal more if we can irrigate the grassland plain to the south of the hills. That's what the dam's for. We can divert a good deal of the river's flow westward into the dry land. At the moment, the grassland's inhabited by nomadic herdsmen—there were a lot of the same type in the plain to the north of the range of hills, and there still are, although farmers are moving in. There's always trouble in that region between herdsmen and farmers, and I think that has a lot to do with the discontent that's bred this vile rumor.

125

"Anyhow, most of my workers come from the villages north of the hills. A couple of months ago I tried to recruit more, and couldn't. Not only that, but once I'd made the trip the rate of desertion on the job itself began to climb. It turned out that there'd been an outbreak of some disease north of the hills, and it was being whispered about that it had been caused by the involvement of local people with the dam—or, more specifically—with me. The herdsmen had always had the disease in their tribes, but it had always been rare. There'd never been an epidemic—only isolated cases. They associated the change with all the other changes going on around them—with the farmers coming, with the road, with the soldiers—all the things which they see threatening their way of life. The trouble is that the farmers seemed to accept this diagnosis, because *they* began to catch the disease too . . . only in ones or twos to start with, but with cases becoming more frequent. The army was infected, too . . . and they *all* began to accept the logic of its being caused by the changes in their way of life. Only the empire immigrants knew that it wasn't *they* who were to blame but *us* . . . the humans. We, in their minds, were the ultimate cause of all the changes. We had been hailed as ilah'y'su by the priests. Thus the disease was the judgment of Y'su, sent because the priests had made a mistake.

"At first I intended to brazen it out. But I couldn't get the work done. The dam was virtually stalemated . . . and then they actually began sabotage. Not only weren't we making progress, but our work was being destroyed. I knew it was only a matter of time before they got to me, too. I had army protection, but I couldn't be wholly sure of their loyalty.

"I'd sent letters here warning of the situation, but I got no reply but reassuring noises from Piet. The rumor hadn't reached Ak'lehr then, and the situation seemed anything but serious to him. I understand things are a little different now, but of course he blames that on me.

"I could see only one thing to do. I had to get out, but getting out wouldn't be enough. I'd leave behind me a flourishing whispering campaign and the possibility of a rebellion in the province. So I decided that the best thing to do was to bring back some of the herdsmen who'd had the disease and recovered—it kills about half of those who catch it—plus some bodies for post-mortem. Here, I thought, we might be able to learn what the disease is and prepare some kind of anti-serum in order to provide immunization. I brought some of the animals, too, because I thought they might be the ultimate cause of the disease if the herdsmen had known it sporadically since time immemorial.

"Well, it seemed like a good plan, but you can imagine the trouble. I had the corpses packed in ice, but it's one hell of a long way from the far south to Ak'lehr. It was a long battle trying to keep the bodies from putrefying. I had to jettison the original ones . . . but then I found that the disease was also traveling north along the road. I got new bodies . . . and had to abandon them, too. I really began to appreciate the magnitude of the problem when I found yet another replacement. Only one, this time . . . but by this time I was deep into the heartland of the empire. This thing is spreading north, and its spreading quickly. Inevitably, the rumor began to grow around me, and with it the rumor that *I* was carrying it . . . that it was me, dragging plague-ridden corpses and herders and their filthy animals, that was spreading the disease. It was useless to point out that it had preceded me to the points where I'd picked up fresh corpses. It was useless to point out that it had been rife long before I set out. Thank Y'su, the soldiers I had with me were sensible men . . . they knew what I was trying to do. They realized the importance of trying to stop this thing. If only Piet realized!

"They wouldn't let me into the city. Rumor had got here ahead of me, and they were certain that if they let my wagons in the plague would be in Ak'lehr itself. Eventually, after half a dozen people from the college came out to talk to me—including Christian—I was allowed in. The wagons are still outside the walls but the rumor is inside and picking up force with every back alley it goes down. Piet's blazing mad . . . but he doesn't see that if I hadn't done what I did I'd have been postponing the day rather than preventing it. This epidemic isn't going to be

127

stopped by ignoring it. We need to take some kind of action . . . at least to find out what's causing it. I think I can persuade some of the masters—they don't like the rumors any more than we do. But the way Piet's acting he's likely to add fuel to the fire instead of water. Christian hasn't told me much about you, except that you're from Earth, but if you can help. . . ."

I nodded. "I can help," I said. "I lost a lot of my equipment in a little domestic dispute, but I have the essentials . . . and the college presumably has its own labs and some kind of facilities. The essential thing is to bring your specimens in and isolate them somewhere. We need help. Are you sure you can get some measure of cooperation from the masters?"

"I can," said Christian. "I've helped out in medical research before. I can get cooperation now. The masters want to stop this plague in the south as much as anyone. They'll take care of the oafs at the gate."

"Then move," I said. "We'd better not waste any time."

Christian nodded, and went to the door. Charles hesitated, then made a small gesture of thanks in my direction, and followed.

I remained seated for a few moments, looking at Jan, who was staring at me pensively.

"Maybe it was a mistake," he said.

"Charles bringing the herdsmen and the body back?" I queried.

"No," he said. "That was criminally stupid. I'm talking about my bringing *you* here."

I shook my head. "What Charles said about postponing the evil day is right," I said. "In either case. He was right to do as he did, and so were you. You have to face things. You can't brush them under the carpet. If you postpone evil days all you gain is a little time—and you lose any chance you ever had of dealing with them when they come."

"It's done now," he said, dismissing the whole issue.

"That's right," I replied. "You'd better come with me to get my equipment—you can show me where the lab is and help me carry the stuff down."

"Do you think you can do anything?" he asked.

"I'm certain."

"Do you think . . . if you hadn't been here . . . we, or the masters . . .?"

"Maybe," I said. "But we'll never know. I can do it better. If there ever was a problem made just for me, then this is it."

"That's what I thought," he said. He still seemed reluctant to move, as if there were still something on his mind.

"What is it?" I asked.

"Nothing," he replied.

"Ilah'y'su," said Mariel, for the first time. "That's it, isn't it?"

He looked at her in some surprise. I realized what she meant. Jan was at least half a believer. He'd been brought up in an alien culture with an alien god. He was his father's son . . . but he was also an Ak'lehrian. He *was* prepared to acknowledge us as messengers of god. Not to the Ore'l, but to *him*.

"Let's go," I said. "There's work to do."

20

I worked all day and most of the night on the body that Charles had brought in. Mariel, Christian and Charles acted as my assistants. We thought it best to keep the masters and all the students who habitually used the lab out of the way, because of the danger of infection. They were not too reluctant to comply.

It was easy enough to find out what—in terms of physical symptoms—had killed the alien. His blood had been poisoned by a reaction rather like hepatitis. Finding the cause was a different matter, with only a small microscope to help. I took blood samples from the herdsmen who'd had the disease and recovered, and then dispatched Christian to get blood samples from some healthy Ore'l. It was a long, slow job. Long before I gave up I knew that Charles' efforts had probably been in vain, at least as far as the dead man was concerned. He had been too long dead, and despite the ice-pack the processes of decay had made my job too difficult.

I got Charles to comb the shaggy fur of the beasts he had brought in, and showed Christian how to prepare blood samples from them for later examination. During breaks in the routine I questioned the herdsmen, with Charles' aid. I formed several hypotheses, and sorted out the one which I felt in my bones to be the likeliest, but I couldn't find anything that looked like definite evidence. I couldn't confidently exclude any of half a dozen possible explanations.

Jan brought food to us during the day, and in the evening he was joined by Anna. She asked probing questions about what we'd found, and I knew she'd be reporting back to Piet. I didn't imagine that the absence of good news would cheer him up, even though it did suggest that he had been right regarding the folly of Charles' action.

I was feeling very disappointed by midnight, and the

others who'd worked with me were sharing the disappointment in full measure. There was a certain desperation in Charles' attempt to find something else we could do that *might* point the way to an answer.

While we sat in dispirited silence, just about ready to pack it in for the night, Jan came into the lab again. He looked at the dissecting table, which was now bare, and at the benches where we'd examined set after set of slides, which were now in a state of tired disarray.

"Nothing?" he asked.

I answered with the slightest of gestures.

"What's the one thing you need in order to crack the problem?" he asked.

At first thought it was a hypothetical problem, and I considered that the answer was so obvious that I could treat it as a rhetorical one. Then I realized that if it was rhetorical it probably wasn't hypothetical.

Charles knew, too. He went white.

"Oh no. . . ." he said, sickly.

"One of the soldiers who brought you back," said Jan. "And he's been off duty for six hours. Most of the time he was at home, but. . . ."

The plague was in the city.

Immediately, I cursed myself for a fool for not insisting that the whole of Charles' returning party should be quarantined. But I had forgotten about the military escort. Had I gone to the city gate myself I would have seen them, or seen *something* that would have triggered the thought in my mind, but I hadn't.

"Where is he?" I asked.

"Upstairs," said Jan. "The hospital wing."

"Can you have the others rounded up?" I asked. "Quarantine them all."

"I'll try," said Jan. "The masters will see the sense in it. But out there. . . ."

Out there, in the city, it only took one event to feed all the rumors with exactly the fuel they'd thrive on.

"Get up there," I said to Christian. "Take the samples. I'll clear the decks here. How bad is he?"

The last sentence was addressed to Jan. "Sick," said Jan. "High fever."

131

Mariel," I said, "try to bring his temperature down. Just do what you can to treat the symptoms. You can handle that?"

She nodded, and left with Christian. I got busy at the bench.

"How serious is it?" asked Jan.

"I can't tell," I said. "It depends how long the disease has been incubating in his blood. If it's just a delayed reaction and he caught it down south, maybe there's no danger at all. But if he caught it near here . . . it all depends on how he caught it. If there's a vector involved, there's no immediate danger. If it can be transmitted from person to person . . . there could be a disaster."

"Can you prepare a serum to combat it?"

"Probably," I replied. "But not in any quantity. I haven't the facilities. And what kind of a serum is possible depends very much on what kind of agent is causing the disease. I suspect some kind of protozoan, but so far I can't rule out bacteria or viruses. . . . until I can plate out blood samples and get a look at them under the microscope I won't be able to tell."

"How long will it take?" asked Charles.

"Maybe a couple of days, maybe a week, maybe. . . ." I ended the statement with a shrug. I set him to prepare more media for plating the blood samples.

"Anything I can get you?" asked Jan.

"Yes," I told him. "A map."

"A map?"

"The best one you have. I want a map of the territory where Charles was working, and of the territory covered by the road connecting it to the nearer reaches of the empire. As much detail as you have."

He didn't ask any more questions. Christian returned, without Mariel, carrying four phials each containing a few milliliters of blood.

Work resumed, with even more urgency than we had mustered during the day.

This time, armed afresh, it was easy. The feeling I already had told me exactly what to look for, and now that I had something to look at it didn't take long. Confirmation, of course, would need a lot more work and some careful handling of the material, but my confidence was high.

Jan had waited, having brought the maps, and it proved not to be too long a wait. As soon as I had it clear in my mind I deserted the microscope for the table. We laid out the maps where earlier in the day the body had lain.

"Show me the migration routes that the herdsmen follow," I asked of Charles.

"North or south of the hills?" he asked.

"North."

With his hand he drew a broad circle. "It's in that area," he said. "I don't know exactly. Maybe the herdsmen can tell us, but they won't understand the map. I'll have to question them . . . and they're sleeping now."

"It's okay," I said. "The southern limit is the forest, here, right? These hills form a long barrier to the south, a kind of base to the whole migratory region . . . the northern herdsmen don't cross?"

"No," said Charles. "Before we took the road through and cleared the forest from this valley here, there were only paths in the forest. There were people in the forest—bandits, according to the nomads. South of the range, of course, there are more herdsmen with different animals, but they're much more scattered and they don't move about as much. They wander from place to place, but as far as I know they don't have settled migration routes."

"These two areas of grassland were separated for thousands of years," I said. "Until you took the road through."

"*Some* people moved across," objected Charles. "I've exaggerated the clearness of the picture. There's always been contact, however tenuous, across the range."

"Some *people* moved across," I said, correcting his emphasis. "But the road opened up a clear gap. You cleared the forest all the way through these valleys, yes?"

"We had to clear land on either side of the road . . . the bandits. And we had to get timber to carry south."

"You opened up a causeway," I said. "Between two isolated regions. You gave the *fauna* of each region access

133

to a new habitat. Previously, the forest and the hills had been a barrier—not to men or to birds or to some of the larger animals, but a barrier nonetheless. A barrier to insects."

"But the plague didn't originate in the south!" Charles protested. "It originated north of the hills, and the disease has always been known north of the hills. There's just never been an epidemic before. I don't see what the south has to do with it . . . we didn't have any cases at all at the dam."

"The flies didn't bring the disease with them," I said. "I say flies . . . it might have been some other kind of bloodsucking insect. The flies just came themselves. When a species first moves into a new suitable habitat it often enjoys a spectacular success. The bloodsuckers from the south probably underwent a population explosion in the north, out-competing the local species that filled the same niche. Probably, the southern species were at an advantage because they're adaptable—they'll suck virtually anyone's blood, while the northern ectoparasites are more specific.

"Anyhow, what I think has happened is that there appeared a transfer mechanism that didn't exist before—out of the south came a vector capable of transmitting a disease endemic in the herdsmen's animal populations—which doesn't do the animals any lasting harm—into the Ore'l population. Ore'l had caught the disease before, but only under odd circumstances—direct contact with the blood of the beasts. Now, there's a convenient vector for carrying the infection from person to person, from animal to person, from person to person, from animal to person, from person to animal . . . you see the pattern?"

"Can you prove this?" asked Charles.

"Probably," I said. "I've already found the organism causing the disease—it's a one-cell creature comparable with Earthly trypanosomes. It's in the blood of the animals you brought back as well as the soldier's. I've deduced the existence of the vector, but an expedition to the south ought to find that particular piece of the jigsaw with no difficulty."

134

"There's no time for that," put in Jan. "Can you cure the disease?"

I shook my head. "I can't effectively muster resources for a massive immunization program, even if I could make a serum," I told him. "Not here. But there's one thing we can be sure of, and that's that the danger isn't immediate here in the city. The soldier must have picked up the disease a long way back on the road—this kind of parasite can lay dormant a long time."

"That's something," said Christian.

"It's a temporary respite," I told him. "Your methods of farming, relying as they do on considerable waterworks to irrigate land, will make things easy for the vector. The disease is already coming north. When it gets beyond the region where the herdsmen carry it around there's always domestic livestock of half a dozen kinds, and there's always the Ore'l. There's no way of telling how much trouble the empire is in for in the long term. Maybe the cooler climate will set a limit on the vector's range. Maybe other ecological factors will stop it. But one thing is certain, and that's that this epidemic is going to kill one hell of a lot of people in the south, and how far north its depredations will spread year by year is anybody's guess. The panic here in Ak'lehr may not last . . . but that isn't going to solve the problem. No way."

"We must be able to do *something*," insisted Charles. "Immunization of some kind . . . show that at least we're fighting this thing."

"You're asking for a medical miracle," I said. "No one can deliver it here."

I put slight emphasis on the word *here*—enough to make Jan ask: "What are you getting at?"

"On Lambda," I said, "there's a starship with a genetic engineering lab. In that lab I can make a medical miracle—not an immunity serum but a tailored virus that will knock out the disease-parasite. It's fighting fire with fire—a bug to exterminate a bug. If I can make that virus and release it in the southern provinces . . . the epidemic would be rapidly checked, and inside two years you wouldn't have a problem at all."

There was silence.

Jan and Christian exchanged a long look.

Charles said: "Piet isn't . . ."

He halted as Mariel entered the room.

"The fever's passed," she announced. "He's still unconscious, but he's not on the danger list as far as I can tell. You'd better come have a look at him."

I nodded, and went without delay. I left the three brothers behind me. None of them followed. They had things to discuss.

I left them to it.

21

I was woken by a hand touching my shoulder. I didn't want to wake up, and I had to force my eyes open to see who it was. It was Jan.

"What time is it?" I asked, feeling that I had to say something if only to force my mind to work.

"Five," he said, meaning late afternoon.

I couldn't work out how many hours of sleep I'd had, but I knew it wasn't enough.

"Ik'ri wants to see you," said Jan, in answer to my unspoken question. "He's with Ur'shere and Ul'el. They want to talk about the plague."

"Where's Mariel?" I asked, shoving the bedclothes back and pulling myself up.

"Asleep. Christian's with the soldier, but he's all right now. He'll recover—but we're keeping him away from other Ore'l for safety's sake."

I began to pull on my clothes. "It might be a lot safer if you put him back in the charge of his own kind," I remarked. "Let them see he's okay and spread the word. If we hold him under our care it's only going to add to the rumors."

He made a slight sound that was partly a laugh and partly an exclamation of disgust.

"The rumors need no adding to," he said. "And there's no spreading the word against them. Do you know how many people die every day in Ak'lehr? Do you know how many of those deaths are being blamed on the plague today? The causes are all different, all familiar . . . but that doesn't stop it. The word is enough . . . somebody dies, whisper it . . . there's no holding it back. In the popular version of the story that soldier's already dead, and if we rode him through the city in the king's carriage no one would believe that he isn't. We've been advised not to go out of the college. I think it's good advice. It's three months since our last riot—there's been one brewing for some time, just waiting for an excuse and a place to happen."

I finished dressing, and reflected that I'd missed breakfast yet again.

"It'll pass," I said. "Without a real epidemic, the panic can't last."

"It'll pass," agreed Jan. "If Ul'el doesn't manage to persuade his fellow magisters that they ought to seize the opportunity to be rid of us. Rid of Piet, anyhow. . . ."

"You think he'll do that?" I asked. Jan held the door open for me, and I went through, waiting in the corridor for him to guide me to my meeting with the aristocracy of Y'su's church.

"He'll try," said Jan. "But I don't think he'll succeed. It would reflect too badly on the church. They're very careful to protect their image. No one in power stands to gain much from any kind of upheaval. Ik'ri and Ur'shere between them can hold Ul'el in check. And with his co-operation they can hold the rest. And who knows—maybe this new popular interest in disease will result in the rebuilding of the city sewers. Charles can abandon his dam and do some real work."

I couldn't make out whether he was covering up his anxiety with the sarcasm or whether he was really sure of himself. I decided upon the former. He was still worried about his own part in the affair, bringing Mariel, Nieland and myself into Ak'lehr.

We eventually came out of the endless maze of corridors into a small courtyard planted with four diamond-shaped flower-beds and a number of young trees. The sun was still high enough in the sky to cast shadows across the paved area at the end where we entered without shading the beds themselves. The three masters were waiting on the benches in the center of the courtyard. I presumed that the meeting-place had been deliberately chosen to emphasize the informality of the occasion.

Jan introduced me to the two who I hadn't previously met, and then left. Within moments of his leaving I had forgotten who was who. They were similarly dressed, and their features all seemed to have a similar cast. I knew which of the three was Ul'el, but for some minutes while the conversations consisted of polite formalities I couldn't separate the other two. They didn't stay still, but moved around as they spoke. Then Ul'el referred to Ik'ri by name, and I grasped the opportunity to keep track of his movements thereafter, though I looked in vain for some feature by which to distinguish him from his colleague.

To begin with, we talked of nothing but generalities and matters of information they must already have had. They were sizing me up. I gathered that they had already talked to Nieland earlier in the day.

Eventually, though, they reached the matter in hand.

"With the aid of the ship that brought you here from Earth you can provide a cure for the disease that is spreading from the south," said the one I was pretty sure was Ik'ri. It wasn't a question.

"I can wipe out the disease-parasite," I said. "That's not quite the same thing as curing individual cases. What I propose to do is actually to make a virus—or to incorporate new genetic material into already-existing viruses—that will attack the parasite. The disease-organism will then suffer itself from an epidemic of plague. It will not be entirely obliterated, but there will be an equilibrium established which will never permit the disease-organism to undergo another population explosion. The disease will still exist—but it is not beyond your resources to come up with medicines for treating the symptoms in individual cases. You should be able to cut the mortality rate greatly."

"How long would this take?" asked Ur'shere.

"That's the worst of it," I said soberly. "Jan's ship can almost certainly get us back to the colony. But the *Daedalus* itself can't fly around in a gravity well—near the surface of the planet, that is. If we're to complete our mission we have to go directly on to the next world. So *Ilah'y'su* will have to bring us back again—or the virus, at least. It can be stored and shipped in crystalline form, so there'll be no problem in handling it, but it will take time. It took the *New Hope* more than a hundred days to make the journey. For *Ilah'y'su* to go both ways it may take a

139

hundred and eighty. She's a slower ship, I think, but going from west to east she'll have the prevailing wind to help her."

"A hundred and eighty days," echoed Ul'el.

"And another hundred for me to make the virus," I said. "It's not easy work. I may be able to do it in less, but I can't guarantee it. The whole process can't take less than half a year . . . and it's likely that you won't get your answer until next spring. I can't work miracles . . . or, if I can, I can't work them instantaneously."

"In that time," said Ul'el, "a great many will die."

"There's nothing can prevent that," I said. "There are precautions—you can make war on the vector that is transmitting the parasite, you can get better medical care to the people in the south. It should be possible to find treatments that are effective to some degree in individual cases. But there is nothing that will stop the epidemic this summer. Until the winter kills the flies you can only fight a rearguard action against the disease."

"If indeed, it cannot be defeated. . . ." said Ik'ri, half to himself. He didn't follow through with the thought, but it was easy enough to understand the way his mind was working. To him, this was indeed a visitation from Y'su. He knew and understood what had happened—about all the causes of the disease. But in his world view it still remained to ask *why*. Why did the parasite exist at all? Why this curious geographical accident that had permitted it to get out of hand? Why *now* and not some other time? We are prepared to shrug our shoulders and acknowledge the role of chance, but in the Ore'l world view there was no such thing as chance. There was only Y'su . . . and his messengers. And, of course, his messages.

Ik'ri wanted to know what Y'su was trying to tell him by setting up the configuration of events in precisely this way and no other. It wasn't an easy problem.

"Why must you return to your ship?" asked Ur'shere. "Why can you not work here?"

"I haven't the equipment," I answered.

"We will make it for you," he said, as if it were the simplest thing in the world.

I shook my head. "You cannot. It will be hundreds of

years before you can make the kind of machines required. Even under the guidance of men who know what is to be done and how. Knowledge is only a part of progress. There must be machines to make machines to make more machines, and machines to make machines to procure what is necessary to make yet more machines. The mind leaps quickly enough from one problem to the next, but the limiting factor is the hand that must do the making. There's a lot of history still in front of you. Empires are not built overnight, as no doubt you know. The time is in the building, not in knowing what to build and how."

Ul'el said something in his own language. I think the others frowned upon his impoliteness. I guessed that what he had said was something along the lines of: "I told you so."

"You are willing to do this for us," said Ik'rī, slowly. "You are willing to help us as the father of the children helped us?"

"Yes," I said.

"And are there conditions attached to your help?" asked Ul'el. Again they might have frowned at him.

I hesitated a little. "Not as such," I said. "I will do what I can to make sure that there is no further outbreak of the disease next year. There's no price for that. I don't want anything in return. But I think it necessary—for your sake as well as the colony's—that this should be the foundation of a friendly relationship between the two continents."

There was a brief silence.

"That is not what Bernhard Verheyden wanted," said Ur'shere.

"Bernhard Verheyden was wrong," I said flatly.

Ur'shere and Ik'ri exchanged a long glance. I could see the irony. In a way, I was almost adding the weight of my argument to the theory that the disease was a judgment of Y'su passed upon the people of Ak'lehr because they had adopted Bernhard Verheyden. They didn't believe that— not in the way that the rumor-mongers believed it—but it was, to them, a plausible "explanation." It was an acceptable way of thinking about the situation, not something that could be declared absurd. I knew full well that I was virtually setting myself up as new messenger from God, delivering a slightly amended version of the last message they'd received. I was doing everything that Piet Verheyden feared that I might—challenging his power and the authority of his father's mission.

It was not the role I would have chosen, but I saw no choice. It had been thrust upon me. There seemed to be no other way to come to terms with the Ore'l. They had to be allowed to think about the situation in their own terms—it would be futile and stupid to try and force them into an alien world view. And if I *could* have myself declared ilah'y'su by the orthodox . . . then surely there was some chance for the establishment of friendly relations between Ak'lehr and the colony. The word of Y'su would be helping instead of hindering.

While I stood there waiting and watching, I realized that it was the only way. While Bernhard Verheyden's voice had been the voice of a god there could be very little hope. That voice had to be replaced by one that would give the Ore'l an attitude that would permit them to approach the matter of contact with the colony constructively and productively.

I looked at Ul'el, and realized that he was pleased. The full significance of what he'd said when I was in his room finally struck me. This was precisely what he wanted. I was his lever to get rid of the Verheyden children. I realized then that he had set me up for this. He had prepared the way for me in advance.

I couldn't help feeling a little frustrated at the way I'd been caught up in the political maneuvering within the college, but everything seemed to be working out. I was relaxing within myself when the next question caught me totally off-balance.

"Where is the ship that brought you here?" asked Ik'ri.

It wasn't just me who was surprised. I could tell by the way he started that this was a new line to Ul'el as well.

I had always avoided the question before, though Jan knew and had presumably passed on the information to his brothers and sister.

There was no reasonable alternative to the truth, so I

142

told it: "The crew of the ship was frightened by its experiences in the forest. They abandoned the three of us and set sail back to the colony."

They did not go back to the colony," said Ik'ri.

I felt a lump in my throat as I tried to speak. Of course they hadn't gone back to the colony. Mariel had done everything in her power to make sure that they *couldn't* go back.

It had seemed like a good idea at the time.

"Where are they?" I asked.

"Sailing north," said Ik'ri. "They have attacked two coastal villages, killing many people. They have guns—the fishermen have none. The humans came ashore to steal food. The fishermen would have given it to them for the asking, but they did not ask. They fired their guns instead."

Ul'el didn't like this kind of surprise. I could see that he was angry. He didn't know whether to be angry at Ik'ri, for not having told him this, or at me. Ik'ri was impassive. I wished I knew how angry he was, inside . . . and whether he intended to blame me.

Silently, I cursed Ogburn many, many times.

"They're frightened men," I said. "They're short of supplies . . . but there's another reason why they're reluctant to go home. They abandoned us—left us for dead. They were reluctant to commit murder, but that's what they were doing, in the final analysis." I took a deep breath. "What you must do is this. The ship will land again—they can't have stolen much from the villages, and ultimately they'll have to make a more definite move. You must watch for her, and send soldiers to the coastal towns. When next she comes to shore, set an ambush. They have very few guns, and they must be very short of ammunition by now. With superior forces and firepower your people will be able to destroy them. That is what you must do."

There was another silence. Ik'ri's eyes never left my face. I kept my expression rigid.

If there was one thing that could make the situation worse and wreck any hope of a sensible outcome to the whole thing it was Ogburn and his merry men attempting

143

to shoot up the empire. If only they'd tried to go home . . . if only Mariel hadn't gone to such lengths to stop them going home. . . .

They had to be destroyed. And I had to sanction their destruction. There was no other way I could hold my position of newly won influence. If I allowed myself to be associated in their minds with Ogburn and his murderous crew then I was finished as a diplomatic force here. If I could have put a stop to the epidemic with an airy wave of the hand it might have been different—I'd have been in a position of real power. But what I was offering was so much less than that—just a chance of stopping *next* year's epidemic. A miracle, maybe . . . but one that had to be taken on trust. They had to trust me for more than half a year while I couldn't show them a single thing in terms of results. If they decided *not* to trust me. . . .

This latest news wasn't going to do a lot for the image of humans in Ak'lehr. If the population was already incensed because it was believed we were spreading plague, the news that a human pirate ship was massacring people up and down the coast was *really* going to stir them up. If Ul'el had waited just one more day he might have found a plan that offered him a much, much easier way of getting rid of the church's human advisors. I knew—and so did he—that Ik'ri had held back this information deliberately.

"And the colony?" asked Ur'shere. "When its masters discover that we have destroyed their people and taken their ship? What will they think of us?"

"Nieland is one of the colony's masters," I told him. "He was one of those left to die. The colony's masters will know that what you did was right. But if you were to return the ship . . . and perhaps capture one or two of the crewmen alive . . . it would all help to smooth things over."

I think the last idiomatic phrase defeated them, but they caught the meaning anyhow.

Ik'ri nodded. *"Ilah'y'su* will sail tomorrow," he said, with an air of finality. I had to take the rest on trust. They were offering no commitments.

But there was one more question I had to ask.

"What about Piet?" I said.

144

"We will take care of Piet," said Ul'el, quietly.

I turned to walk out of the courtyard, ducking under a low branch of one of the ornamental trees. I didn't feel like a man who'd brought off a diplmatic coup. I felt like a man who'd just betrayed two groups of his fellow men. It wasn't much of a consolation being fairly sure that Nathan would be proud of me.

22

There seemed to be a lot to do with what was left of the day. I ate with Nieland, and compared notes about our respective interviews with the magisters. They hadn't mentioned the little matter of the *New Hope* and her coastal raids—they'd been more concerned with sounding him out on the subject of the colony. They had, however, issued an invitation to him to stay in Ak'lehr as long as he cared to. I told him about Ogburn's piratical activities and what I'd advised. He didn't seem in the least bothered by it. He seemed to figure that Ogburn and the crew deserved anything they got. His only concern was for the future of his ship. I assured him that the Ore'l would recover it for him if they got the chance. I tried to impress upon him once again the importance of his role in Ak'lehr, but only succeeded in irritating him. He knew the score now.

After the meal I went back to the labs to begin preparing material for the trip home. I needed samples of blood serum, of dead parasites, and of live animals to provide me with a source of fresh parasites back in the colony. I talked at some length to Jan and Al'ha about arrangements for maintaining the animals on the long voyage. Jan seemed to have accepted the situation as it was. He hadn't seen Piet since I'd talked to the magisters.

Christian helped me to make preparations for the voyage, and so did Mariel when she finally woke up. With one thing and another we were busy just about all evening. I got back to my own room to pack up my personal belongings well after dark.

I wasn't really surprised to find someone waiting for me. I had, in fact, half expected Piet to be there. The only surprise was that it wasn't Piet but Anna.

"Hello," I said, levelly. I think I spoke rather more

loudly than was necessary. She made a gesture that suggested I keep my voice down.

"Why?" I said, in a stage whisper. "Who's listening?"

"Piet has been arrested," she said.

"*Arrested*?"

"He was summoned by Ik'ri. He was with the magisters for a long time. When he came out, he was under guard. Now Charles and Jan have been summoned. Christian and I will presumably be next."

Her voice was low, and she was putting some effort into keeping it level. She didn't speak in the tone of someone imparting information—more as one who demands an explanation.

"I think Piet may have been given an expulsion order," I said, deciding that there was no point in beating about the bush. "I don't know—it's nothing to do with me—but I suspect he's to be sent home. To the colony, that is."

"This is your doing," she said.

"Not the way you mean," I told her. "Though if it *were* my decision, I think I'd do the same. Our coming here merely provided the excuse . . . not even that, simply a convenient opportunity. The Ore'l don't need Piet any more. They haven't needed him for years. And he isn't even useful. Not as useful as Jan, or Charles, or Christian. All they needed was a new way to look at the situation . . . a way that let them off the hook as far as squaring what they wanted to do with what they thought they ought to do. Not just Ul'el, but the others too."

"Are we all to be sent to Lambda on *Ilah'y'su*?" she asked bitterly.

"I don't know," I said. "Nieland has been invited to stay. Jan, at least, will return with the ship. I think Christian will return too—probably as the one who implements the plan I'll be able to set in motion from Lambda. Someone will have to spread the virus to fight the disease. It needn't be me. In many ways, it would be best for one of your family to do it. But it has to be Christian. He'll accept a new definition of his mission here. Piet never would."

"Christian is not of the family," she said, acidly. The bile must really have risen into her throat to make her say

147

it. The venom in her voice directed toward her youngest brother—or half-brother—was as fierce as anything Piet could have mustered.

"I think he feels the same way," I retorted sharply. "Who gave him that scar around his eye?"

She didn't answer. There didn't seem to be all that many possibilities. I wouldn't have needed three guesses.

"What about Jan and Charles?" I asked. "They'll accept the situation, won't they?"

She wanted to deny it—I could see her struggling to produce the denial. But it wouldn't come. She knew only too well that when they came from their conference with the magisters they wouldn't be under guard. They wouldn't have to be. They weren't going to like me for what had happened, but for better or worse they had already taken sides against Piet.

"Jan was a fool," she said. "He should never have brought you here. And Charles. . . ."

"Maybe it was Y'su's will," I said, with the irony setting my voice like steel. I wasn't in the mood to be gentle.

I watched the anger flare up in her face, and then watched it fade away. I was puzzled by the way it faded.

"Is it really such a bad thing?" I said, quietly now. "Did you really want it to go on forever? How can your father's resentment of the colony mean anything to you? Even if he drummed it into you from the moment you were born . . . he might have infected you with it but he could never have made it *mean* anything to you. The colony is where your own people are. Human beings. You can't shut yourself away from the colony forever—it *exists*. It's *there*. You don't have to live there, to be a part of it, but you can't exclude it from your scheme of being. What kind of life do you think this is . . . you and your four brothers a little enclave in an alien society? If that's the way you want it, all right—but at least look at the alternatives. At least be prepared to make contact with other human beings. You *are* human, you know."

The anger rose again within her as I spoke. It came to the boil and died back, but remained—seething and simmering beneath the surface. I could understand it. I was the destroyer, who'd come from outside and turned her world upside down, opening it up to all kinds of possibilities that she'd never considered save in the idlest of dreams. Maybe it *would* be for the best—maybe she could see that it might be—but for the moment she was estranged, frightened, full of anger. . . .

When she stood up I thought she was going to hit me. But as she clenched her fist the impulse was countered by something else. She stood, almost trembling with effort as her feelings conflicted. Out of the conflict came tears—bitter tears that flowed unsteadily.

The feeling of having betrayed them all that had seized me briefly when I walked from the courtyard returned again now, and with it—inevitably—came a measure of remorse.

I stepped forward and put my arms around her, awkwardly. My motives were sincere and my intentions quite honorable.

Once I was holding her it was as if I could feel the emotional turmoil in her body. Her first movement was to thrust me away, but that died quickly, and her arms slipped round beneath mine. Her hands, rigid as gripping claws, clutched at my shoulders and the pressure seemed to be intended to squeeze and hurt, except that. . . .

I realized that the turmoil was more complex than I had thought. There were more feelings than anger and fear and hate. In emotional excess *any* feeling is likely to burst through, because all the controls and inhibitions are off. Not since she was a child had Anna seen a man, save for her brothers. . . .

Inevitably, I responded.

And that was when the door opened, and Piet walked in.

He hadn't bothered to knock. He didn't look to be in the mood for observing the proprieties of etiquette. He looked coldly angry. That is, he looked coldly angry for all of the two seconds before the sight of what we were doing burned an impression upon his brain. Then his face turned crimson.

Anna spun away from me, with an expression on her face that registered a degree of guilt I hadn't known hu-

149

man faces could express. The shock seemed to have upset her as much as it upset Piet.

I wished briefly that Mariel was there to read their faces. In all likelihood there would never be such a moment again. Piet registered horror, fury and—or so it seemed to me—outraged jealousy. Sexual jealousy.

Anyhow, whether that was so or not, he completely lost his mind. Presumably murder had not been in his plans when he entered the room, though it might have been lurking somewhere within his imagination. But there was no doubting as he came at me like a tiger that murder was what he intended now.

He cannoned into me and hurled me over backward. There was a table behind me, on which approximately half the contents of the medical kit I'd brought back from the lab were scattered. I'd just dumped them when I came in to find Anna waiting for me. Now the table went over with a crash and everything on it was thrown to the floor. I went over with a terrible crash, taking the fall on my shoulders. Had my head hit the floor direct I'd have been knocked unconscious, but as it was I just felt a lance of pain shoot through me, and then had to struggle as Piet landed on top of me, his fingers reaching for my throat. I managed to turn him aside and wrenched myself free. My first thought was to get away, and so I leapt back over the table and gripped the legs that jutted into the air, intending to use it as a shield.

It was a mistake on two counts. For one thing the table was so heavy I could barely drag it along the floor, let alone lift it to fend off the maddened Piet. For another, Piet was on the floor amid the scattered contents of the medical kit. Scalpels aren't designed for killing people, but they can be pretty vicious weapons. When he came to his feet he had one in his hand, and there could be no possible doubt as to where he intended to stick it.

I let go of the table and backed away, looking for something I could use to defend myself. All that my groping hand found was the bag in which most of my spare clothes were stashed. I picked it up and held it before me, ready to try and take the cut of the scalpel in its soft bulk.

Piet came forward and I backtracked warily. Neither of us was moving fast. My one intention was to drag the fight out—to stop him cutting me up until he had at least the chance to calm down. Fury such as his can die down as fast as it arises.

He lunged, and I raised the bag to catch the tiny blade.

But I was too slow.

Suddenly, there was someone else between us, and when Piet's arm lashed out with all the force he could muster it wasn't my small bundle that absorbed the thrust but Anna's body.

The blade went into her neck at the side and must have sheared straight through the carotid artery. Her arms were outraised, fingers splayed, in a gesture of prohibition that seemed almost a caricature.

He had not even seen her.

Blood flooded out of the cut, spilling over the shoulder of her dress and the back of Piet's hands. He let go of the scalpel as if stung, and she crumpled to the floor.

For half a second it was an open question whether he'd resume his murderous attack on me or give way to the grief that was trying to displace his fury. But he was a defeated man, and he'd been defeated long before he'd come into the room. He crumpled to his knees, and bent over the prostrate body. Her eyes were open, and she blinked once. But she couldn't say anything, or even change the expression of devastated shock on her face.

She died, still spilling blood all over the floor.

Someone screamed. Not Anna, who had never made a sound, but Mariel, who'd come in to find out what all the noise was about.

Then Nieland arrived. Soon after that there was a crowd. I don't know how death attracts so many people so quickly, but it always seems to.

I threw the bag on the bed with a gesture of utter disgust. Mariel, eyes closed, was clinging hard to Christian. Jan shut the door.

"Why did they let him go?" I asked, my voice caught in a half-whisper.

"He accepted the situation," said Jan. "He asked them

to release him so that he could prepare for the voyage. Nobody thought. . . ."

"No," I said, looking down at the silent form of the stricken Piet. "I don't suppose anyone would."

23

Piet was taken by carriage to the dock downriver of Ak'lehr where *Ilah'y'su* was moored. Anna's body went with him, scheduled for burial at sea. Jan and Charles took charge of the operation, leaving Christian behind.

The three of us gathered in Mariel's room, largely to avoid the smell of blood. I abandoned my packing while Christian found me a stiff drink.

He, strangely enough, seemed relatively unmoved by what had occurred.

"We are all to sail on the ship tomorrow," he said. "We leave early—just after dawn. Only your friend Nieland will remain. Those of us who wish to will be permitted to return with *Ilah'y'su*. By next spring, it will all have been forgotten, and as soon as the sickness breaks out again we will be on hand to defeat it. A small miracle, readily staged. In the meantime, the magisters will appear to have acted in accordance with the popular sentiment, without ever being forced to make any official statement."

"You know that you would have been forced to leave here in any case," I said. "Sooner or later. Ul'el would have had his way. This way is better. For everyone."

"I know that," he said.

"You're glad," said Mariel. "Of all of you, you're the only one who's pleased that it's all happened."

"What do you think?" asked Christian, with a cutting edge in his voice.

She was unperturbed. "You must have been very lonely," she said.

Christian shrugged slightly, and turned away.

"Bernhard Verheyden killed my father," he said, in a deliberately offhand tone. "When he knew that I was not his son. Piet tried to kill me once. The others . . . they always knew that I was different, but they didn't know how they were supposed to behave. They just didn't *know*. I tried to be one of them. I've always tried. But there was never any real chance. I was always excluded, somehow, from the whole thing."

"You will come back?" I said, anxiously. "Someone has to bring the virus. I'd rather it was you."

"I'll come back," he said softly. "Not as Bernhard Verheyden's son. As ilah'y'su. In my own right. As myself. Jan and Charles . . . they haven't really got selves to be. Because they *are* Bernhard Verheyden's sons. And Piet—Piet most of all."

I nodded, not pretending that I agreed, or understood, but merely accepting his declaration of intent.

"We haven't solved anything," said Mariel. She was talking to me, reacting to something she'd picked up in my thoughts.

"What do you mean?" I asked.

"You're accepting all this as if we'd achieved something," she said. "But we haven't. We haven't altered the situation at all. We're no closer now to making any kind of a bridge between the Ore'l and the colony than we ever were."

"Christian is coming back," I said. "Nieland is still here. There's going to be a two-way crossing of the ocean at long last. That's all worth something. It all counts."

"For what? Can you honestly say that what has happened here will measurably influence the history of this world in the slightest degree?"

"We could never be sure of that," I said. "Not even if we could track this world over the next thousand years. But what happened here could have been worse. And it would have been worse if we hadn't been dumped on the doorstep when we were. We arrived at just the right time. A small miracle, in more ways than one. Maybe it'll turn out to be an unnecessary miracle. Maybe a futile one. But don't deny it. I don't say we've achieved something here—we did what was here for us to do. But we did it."

"And with Nathan to write it up for us we can pretend to be masterminds?"

I ignored that particular remark, and tried to find what was really worrying her.

"Do you want to stay here?" I asked. "With Nieland?"

154

She shook her head.

"There isn't a real job to be done here," she said. "Not any more. Everything's already under way."

She felt, in some peculiar way, as if she'd been cheated. It had all happened too quickly. It had happened all around her. It hadn't been as she'd anticipated it at all. She'd been desperate for one more chance to use a power she was so afraid of losing. When the *New Hope* had first come to shore it looked as if she'd been robbed of the chance. When the forest savages picked us up it looked as if she'd got it back. Now . . . the situation had moved far beyond the simple matter of opening communication and learning to understand. All in all, coincidence had served us very well. But from her particular point of view . . . it wasn't a victory, by any means.

"Saving worlds isn't a simple business," I told her. "Sometimes there's a single problem and a single answer. But even when it seems as simple as that there's much, much more. Nothing is guaranteed. Nobody guaranteed you a set of ritual opportunities with ritual answers. You can't expect things to go by a carefully prepared script. We find what we find and we make the best of it. You've seen a good deal of the Ore'l. You'll see a good deal more yet. There's a lot you can learn and it will all be useful. Don't be discouraged because it doesn't fit your preconceived ideas about what ought to have happened. The world doesn't work like that."

Christian didn't know what the hell we were talking about. She took mercy on him and let me change the subject. I was sure she'd come round, in time. At the moment, things looked to be in a hell of a mess.

"The Ore'l will contain the plague this year," I said, aiming at Christian. "With what we were able to find out about it. The magisters will be able to muster some kind of resistance."

Christian let go a dry, humorless laugh. "They will," he said. "I know them. Do you know what they'll do?"

"If they've any sense," I said, "they'll close the road."

"They'll do that," said Christian. "And they'll slaughter every single animal in every single herd within the area of infection. That won't destroy the center of the infection

155

entirely—too many people have caught the disease and the vector can transmit from person to person. But it will help. And it's a good excuse. Their sympathies are with the farmers, you see. There's always been trouble in that region between incoming farmers and the native nomads. This is an excuse for genocide . . . all the while maintaining the church's front of total benevolence."

He said it all quite emotionlessly, with no hint in his tone of moral censure. I took it all in the same way. It was logical. I'd have realized it myself, if only I'd thought.

"There'll be some battles fought," I said.

"The nomads are dying with the plague anyhow," said Christian.

Another phrase echoed in my mind: *"They're only forest savages."*

There was no point in worrying about it. No point even in feeling sick. Attica was a cruel world.

So are they all.

As Mariel said, we hadn't actually *solved* anything. Sometimes, there are no neat answers. You just have to do what the situation allows you to do.

"We'd better get busy," I said. "We still have a lot of packing to do."

24

If our first sea journey on Attica had been an uncomfortable one, the second had all the makings of a nightmare. Piet began the trip locked in his cabin, and that was the way I—at least—intended it to say. Aboard *Ilah'y'su,* however, my authority did not count for a great deal. Here, at least, the Verheydens retained their power. The previous evening, Jan and Charles had reacted quickly enough to the situation which they had found in my room. They had asked no questions. But it only took time for the questions to come floating to the surface, and they wanted answers. Piet told them nothing—which left it all down to me.

The matter came to a head when we all (except Piet) sat down to a late breakfast, and were thus together for the first time. I had not at any time been top of the local popularity poll, and both Jan and Charles were by now harboring strong regrets about ever having become acquainted with me. They suspected that whatever had happened the night before I was more than half responsible.

It was Jan, adopting the lead because he was master aboard his own ship, who asked me what happened. I had already thought about how to reply to such a question, but had not progressed far in the matter of sorting out an ideal—or even an acceptable—answer.

"When Piet was released," I said, "he must have come straight to my room. I don't think he came with the intention of committing murder—more to blow off some steam. I'd had some of that before, after seeing Ul'el. He was waiting for me then to make threatening noises. But when he found Anna. . . ."

"Wait!" Jan interrupted. "What was Anna doing there?"

"She came for the same reason," I said. "To accuse, to

insult . . . just to pay me back a little for what she imagined I'd done."

"Imagined?" queried Charles. But he didn't seem to put any real venom into it.

"She was upset," I said, electing to censor the account somewhat—more (I assured myself) for their benefit than for mine. "I was trying to calm her down. She was crying. I was trying to reassure her. When Piet opened the door and saw us he leapt immediately to the wrong conclusion. He just went mad. He attacked me, and somewhere in the struggle picked up the scalpel. Anna was trying to stop him, trying to make him see sense. But he was just stabbing blindly. He didn't know what he was doing. Until he killed her. And when he *did* realize what he'd done . . . the rest you know."

By the way Jan was looking at me I could tell that while he didn't quite disbelieve me, he was not wholly ready to believe me, either.

"He was trying to kill you?" he said.

"Yes."

"And she was trying to stop him?"

"Yes."

"Anna's my sister," he said. "*Was* my sister. She and Piet . . . well, it seems to me that if Piet had wanted to kill you she'd more likely have helped him than tried to stop him."

"That's a vile thing to say!" said Christian.

Jan transfixed him with a glare. "Why should Anna risk her life for him?" he said. "Is that how *you* see Anna?"

"In the heat of the moment. . . ." said Christian, defensively.

"Why else should Piet kill her?" Mariel intervened. The question cut through the burgeoning family dispute like a knife, challenging the foundations of Jan's suspicion.

He had no answer. At least he didn't want to argue that maybe Piet hadn't done it.

"Look," I said, "I feel pretty bad about this myself. She got killed, if you want to put it like this, instead of me. I don't think she cared about me one way or the other. It was Piet she was thinking about. But she still got herself killed, and possibly saved my life in so doing. How do you think *I* feel? Delighted? Thankful? It hurts, for God's sake . . . it really hurts. And out of that you want to build a family quarrel. What the hell *for*? What kind of people *are* you?"

Jan's eyes flashed with sudden anger—the same sudden anger that seemed to be the curse of all his kin. But he masked it quickly. Long practice of being a younger brother is the ideal trainer in self-control. It may not damp the aggression but it short-circuits the action well enough.

"To the Ore'l," said Jan slowly, "you may be a messenger from Y'su. But what are you to us? In a few short days. . . . How much more is there to come? Can you destroy us all before we reach Lambda? Is any of us ever going to see Ak'lehr again? Have you special seats in hell reserved for the whole family? Tell us, please . . .?"

"Jan," said Christian, softly. "You're talking like a lunatic."

"Like Piet?" asked Jan, his voice jagged with suppressed pain.

"Piet will be all right," said Christian.

"All right!" exclaimed Charles. "How in Y'su's name can he ever be all right? He's lost everything he had, including Anna, whose throat he cut himself in a moment of blind anger. How can he ever be all right? He's under lock and key now—do we have to keep him that way forever, just to protect this one from being murdered?"

The wave of his hand was, of course, directed toward me. Yet again, my temper outweighed my sense of diplomacy. "Wouldn't it be rather a waste," I snapped, "if Anna got killed trying to stop Piet murdering me, and then he went and did it anyhow."

"You killed Anna," said Jan, flatly. "Your coming here. Your determination to interfere. You were the cause of his anger."

"He was the cause of his own anger!" I spat. "His fevered imagination! He thought himself a dictator when he'd long since lost any real power. He thought himself injured when everything that happened was inevitable. He saw Anna and me together and out of his mind flooded all kinds of crazy thoughts. What *I* did was to precipitate a crisis that had been coming for years. What I did was to provide something that might bring together the colony and the empire into a relationship which has at least the prospect of peaceful coexistence. You're so wrapped up in the microcosm of your family loyalties you're blind to the real issues here. Without my arrival, my chance to stop this plague before it takes off again next year and decimates the southern reaches of the empire, what kind of future do you think this world could have had? Piet's policies were heading straight for some kind of confrontation with the colony, and then to war. It's up to you—*all of you*—to do what Anna did and *get in his way*, to try to undo what he's done. You have to get out of the stupid way of thinking your father left you and start thinking about everyone else, human and Ore'l alike. If you can't find another way of thinking during the next half-year, you'll take back to the empire exactly the same seeds of destruction that we have locked up in a cabin right here on board. Can't you for one minute strip away your blinkers and realize the importance of getting this virus back to Ak'lehr and using the opportunity it provides to begin all over again. You can still be ilah'y'su if that's the game you want to play *but the message has to change.*"

The sheer vehemence of the tirade left them somewhat at a loss. Only Christian found words, and what he said was: "He's right."

My speech hadn't been a masterpiece of tact. That brief comment, however grateful *I* was to hear it, was the thing that really killed the argument. It killed the argument because it brought out a stock response—a response I'd already seen in Piet and Anna. It was a formula that allowed Jan to dismiss every last thing I'd said without further contemplation. Instead, he rounded on Christian, and said: "*You* would!"

Every time the chips were down, the sons of Bernhard Verheyden had that ready: the accusation of betrayal, aimed at the brother who was *not* their father's son.

Christian came to his feet, ready to fight. Jan was even readier. Charles stood up too, and I never found out

160

whether he was going to do the sensible thing and try to separate them, or whether he was going to turn it into a free-for-all.

The reason I never found out is that there was a sudden violent knocking on the door. It was thrown open without the benefit of a pause for a reply.

Al'ha's shaggy head appeared in the gap, and he said: " 'Ere's a shi'! We unner a'hack!"

Even as he spoke I heard the muffled crack of a rifle.

"Oh Jesus," I moaned. "It's the bloody *New Hope*. That stupid bastard Ogburn's trying to hijack us!"

25

We paused in the hatchway that opened up on to the deck. There had been no more firing, but no one was eager to rush out and make a target of himself. I could see the tops of the *New Hope*'s masts away to port, and though they seemed close I suspected that she was out of range. *Ilah'y'su* was in the process of trying to tack away to starboard.

Al'ha went up first, keeping low and making for the cover of the bridge. Jan followed, and then the rest of us, one by one. I expected Mariel to stay below, but when I turned around after reaching cover she was right behind me. We were crammed into the wheelhouse, and it was pretty crowded. Al'ha took the wheel and told the Ore'l who'd been steering to stand by and keep low.

The *New Hope* was also coming about to follow us.

"What does he think he's doing?" I muttered. "First he raids coastal villages—now he's attacking ships at sea. We can't be more than a couple of miles out from land in the middle of the empire."

"He doesn't know there's an empire," Mariel reminded me. "I always had him down as a frustrated pirate."

"Hail him," said Jan, to me. "Tell him who we are. Maybe we can make him change his mind."

"No chance," I muttered, under my breath. Aloud, I said: "It might come better from you. If he sees me or Mariel he's going to start worrying about past crimes."

Jan nodded. He stepped out of the wheelhouse and vaulted up on to its roof, supporting himself against the mainmast.

"Hey!" his voice boomed out. "Hold your fire!"

He must have been clearly visible. He was just as clearly human. It must have come as something of a surprise to Ogburn and his crew. The *New Hope* was a bigger, faster ship, and she was managing to keep almost

162

abreast of us, though some thirty degrees or so to the rear, and I could see a couple of men up in the rigging looking down at us. I kept my head down, making absolutely certain I couldn't be identified.

There was a long pause while Ogburn discussed the new development with his officers.

"What weapons do we have aboard?" I asked Al'ha.

He shrugged. "Cross'ows," he replied.

"They can't have many rifles," I mused. "And hardly any ammunition if they've been shooting up the coastal villages. Lots of knives and the like—plus my dart gun. But given the advantage of our crewmen in hand-to-hand encounters, I reckon we can. . . ."

Then a nasty thought struck me.

"You threw the contents of the armory overboard?" I said to Mariel.

"Most of it," she confirmed. "But there were at least half a dozen guns ashore, with some ammunition."

"And then you went to the hold?"

"That's right."

"You didn't by any chance abstract from there the case containing the dynamite?"

"Oh!" she said. "No. No, I didn't."

"In that case," I said, "we'd better pray that they haven't rigged up a catapult." It was meant to be a joke, however feeble. All they'd *really* need would be a man who could throw an object weighing a couple of hundred grams a couple of hundred feet. Not difficult.

The *New Hope* was edging closer. Jan was still on top, waiting for an answer. It came in the form of a loud *crack*! and a little dart that struck the outer rail of the ship. It missed Jan by twenty feet, but it was the thought that counted. I decided that it was no use pretending any longer, and I swung myself out of the wheelhouse up on to the roof to join Jan.

"*Ogburn!*" I yelled, still kneeling and trying to get some of the bulk of the mast between myself and the *New Hope*. "What do you think you're doing?"

Ogburn had never been a talkative man. The next dart struck the wheelhouse only half a meter from my hand. I jumped down to the deck, and Jan jumped with me. He

163

shouted a stream of orders in the language of Ak'lehr, and Al'ha spun the wheel to turn us away. Someone went below, presumably to mobilize our defenses, such as they were.

"No firearms at all?" I asked Jan.

"The army has first call on firearms," he said dryly. "The entire supply is brought up as it leaves the factories. It's a big army and it keeps busy."

"Why is he attacking us?" asked Charles, from the shadow of the wheelhouse.

"Because he's scared," I replied. "He's found out that the empire is bigger than he is, even though he has no idea *how* big. He wants to go home. My guess is he daren't try to raid on shore any more, so he intends to plunder local shipping. The fact that there are humans aboard doesn't alter his plan one way or the other. He must be pretty desperate."

"If it comes to a fight," said Jan, "we can win."

"It *is* a fight," I assured him. "But we're going to have to play dirty to stop him using the explosives. We're going to have to offer to surrender. Offer him our supplies—once he knows we're fitted out for an ocean voyage he'll have to bargain. It's his best chance of getting home. He won't mean it, we won't mean it . . . but we can both pretend long enough to get us into a better position. Get your men ready, Jan. I'll do the talking."

All the while the *New Hope* was taking the best of our wind. She was only forty or forty-five meters adrift of us, though she was almost directly behind us now, rocking in our wake. At any time she could drift to one side and come up abreast of us again, but Al'ha kept us turning while he could. There was only so far we could go without losing the wind altogether and setting ourselves up as sitting ducks. We only had minutes to play with—theirs was the better ship and they were probably the better sailors.

I edged my way toward the stern, to get into a better position to hail the *New Hope*. Nobody followed me.

"Ogburn!" I shouted. "Hold your fire. We're unarmed. If you sink us you'll lose our supplies. We have all your instruments and supplies for a journey to Lambda. You

164

can have it all if you'll let us go back to the rivermouth unharmed."

That sounded like a reasonable proposition for an unarmed idiot to make. Ogburn would murder us anyhow, but if he thought we were at his mercy he might think we were stupid enough or desperate enough to try to buy him off. The prospect of getting Nieland's instruments and all our food—not to mention his compass needle—must have really made his mouth water.

"Heave to, then!" came an answering voice. "We won't hurt you. Get the supplies and the instruments into your boats. We'll take it aboard. Then you can go back."

I expressed my true feelings about that statement with succinct disgust, but silently. I shouted back instant agreement.

Jan shouted more orders, and we came about to port, letting the *New Hope* come broadside on again. Long minutes passed while they maneuvered into the position they wanted. They didn't approach much closer than they already had. They were taking no chances. There was less than fifty meters between the two ships, though. And we were unobtrusively drifting closer.

"Come on!" howled the man in the rigging of the *New Hope*. "Start loading your boats! Move it, or we start shooting!"

I moved back to stand beside Jan. We both stood clear of cover, as though accepting the situation. Along the deck, several Ore'l were poised out of sight, with crossbows ready. We couldn't move them right up to the bulwarks, or even into any position from which they'd be able to move with the requisite speed. They were just too big.

"Take it slowly," I said. "Inch by inch."

"Al'ha knows what he's doing," he replied.

He barked out further orders, and a couple of crewmen emerged from the hold carrying casks and boxes. They placed them ostentatiously in the boat on the port side—facing the *New Hope*. Jan and I went below with them, and Charles and Christian joined us. With six of us working it wouldn't take very long to load up the boat, but it

165

would take at least three trips to transfer the stuff from one ship to the other. It wasn't a very big boat.

When I brought out my second load I could see that the gap between the ships had shrunk perceptibly. And now there was an Ore'l, with a bolt already fitted to his crossbow, crouched in the shadow of the boat. As we carried the bulky bundles out of the hold we provided a shield for two more to get into the same position.

"Use the other boat!" shouted the man relaying Ogburn's orders. He was dangerously close, now—he was only a few meters up in the rigging, but soon he'd be able to see too much as he looked down and across at the deck of *Ilah'y'su*. Next time I went below I took Mariel with me.

"Get ready," I said to Jan, as I paused just beneath the hatchway.

Jan looked out over the rim, judging the nearness of the other ship. He called out to Al'ha in a perfectly normal voice, safe in the knowledge that the crew of the *New Hope* couldn't understand a word. Then he picked up a bundle and walked slowly out to the boat, letting Ogburn's men watch him every inch of the way.

Al'ha swung the wheel, and we headed straight for the *New Hope* on a collision course.

They opened fire.

I kept my head down and waited out the long, long seconds. At any moment there might be a bang loud enough to spell destruction. But none came. They had been too confident. Bullets and darts hit the wood of the deck and the wheelhouse, but did no damage at all. Arrows crossed the water in the other direction, and the man on the rigging tumbled from his post, screaming.

The time seemed to drag on forever while we cut on and on through empty water. And then there was an appalling grinding sound as the timbers of the two ships met. Howling like a madman Jan leapt from cover behind the loaded boat and led his crewmen leaping across the sealed gap. Our men came out from everywhere, firing as they came and fighting to get an opportunity to board the enemy. I don't know how many got across before the gap opened again, but it must have been seven at least, and one who didn't make it landed in the water and began to swim through the loose weed to clamber up the side of the *New Hope*.

Charles and Christian, with three more Ore'l, began lowering the boat, hurling out the casks and boxes as they did so. They worked so furiously that they had all but unloaded her in the half-minute before she was too low for them to hurl more back on *Ilah'y'su*'s deck. It hit the water with a great splash, and they too were off to join the fight.

The reinforcements, I knew, would be desperately needed, although it was impossible to tell exactly how the battle on the *New Hope's* deck was going. All was chaos, with the sound of guns going off mingling with shouts and howls of pain and anguish.

As the boat turned to begin its journey one more crewman jumped over the side to join it. Then another figure appeared by my side and without a moment's pause followed him. It was Piet, apparently as savagely keen to get into the fight as anyone else. I saw Charles haul him out of the water into the bobbing boat, which lurched and spun before resuming its passage across the gap that was widening with every second that passed.

I moved back into the shelter of the wheelhouse, now inhabited only by Al'ha. He looked at me with an unfathomable expression. I couldn't tell whether he was censuring me for not joining in the riot. I wasn't really sure why I hadn't. It had simply never occurred to me to do so.

Mariel suddenly appeared by my side again.

"You should have stayed below!" I hissed.

"Can't see what's happening," she replied.

"Los' win' now," muttered Al'ha, who was still trying to turn the ship toward the *New Hope* and keep us as close as possible. Despite his efforts the gap kept getting wider. There was twenty meters of clear water, now. But the boat had reached its destination, and humans and Ore'l alike were clambering up the side of the *New Hope* to get into the fight. Only one of the Ore'l was carrying a crossbow—the rest had big knives like machetes—even Piet. I guessed that they must have been transferred to

the boat ready for the attack, in with all the other inno-
cent bundles.

When the reinforcements joined in the chaos seemed to
abate somewhat. No guns were firing now—there had
been no opportunity for anyone to reload. It was all
blades and claws, and on that basis the colony men didn't
stand a chance.

Five minutes, I knew, would have it won.

But then I looked directly across into the bridge of the
New Hope, and saw the one thing that I feared most of
all. I could see Ogburn, not calling orders, not even getting involved in the fight.

He was setting a light to a fuse dangling from a
greasy-gray cylinder, and with perfect calmness he sighted
it at me. Our eyes met, and in that exchanged glance
there was perfect understanding of the whole situation.

He raised his arm, aiming at the wheelhouse. It was a
throw that anyone could have made, and I knew him well
enough to know that his aim was going to be good.

I tried to push Mariel out of the wheelhouse on the
starboard side, but I was thrusting backward with my
arms and making no effort to move myself. I just couldn't
take my eyes off Ogburn, and I had the sensation of being
able to read his very thoughts as he went through the act
of killing me.

And then something rose from the deck beneath his
steady arm . . . something that was already stained with
blood from a blow with an axe that had ripped apart its
left shoulder. It was Piet Verheyden, and his machete was
already raised high, the sunlight flashing from its blade
into my eyes.

Piet stabbed with all the strength of his one good arm,
and as the blade went into Ogburn's belly my mind's eye
flashed a recapitulated image of a scalpel slicing into
Anna's neck. Then I had to look away because of the
dazzling flash of reflected sunlight.

I had no idea whether Ogburn had made his throw or
not. I just dropped to the deck, still pushing at Mariel and
pulling at Al'ha.

I remember saying: "Get down!" in as loud a voice as

I could, and repeating it as many times as I could before. . . .

There was one small bang.

That was the stick of dynamite Ogburn had intended to throw.

Then there was a big bang.

That was the rest of the case.

The small bang must have demolished the *New Hope's* bridge. The large one blew the heart clean out of the ship.

It took a long time for the booming in my ears to die away. Until it had, I wasn't sure what had happened, or which ship had blown, or whether the rest of me was still attached to my head.

Eventually, though, it was over, and I felt the awesome relief of wholeness.

Al'ha, who had not dropped to the floor but had at least shielded his head with a furry forearm, said: "Blurry hell!"

"Don't worry," I said, weakly. "No need to fret. They were only savages . . . only savages."

26

In the evening, I made the rounds of my various patients. We had picked up a reasonable number of survivors—mostly Ore'l. It had never before occurred to me to consider the advantages of light fur as a protection against blast-burns, but on comparing the injuries of the aliens with the humans we picked up I had to admit that it was a point well worth considering. I came to the conclusion that if God had intended us to invent dynamite he would never have allowed evolution to strip us naked first.

Only two of Ogburn's crew had failed to go down (or up, if one considers the explosion rather than the eventual fate of what was left of the *New Hope*). One was Malpighi, who had one broken leg and some unpleasant but not particularly desperate second-degree burns. The other was Thayer, who had been somewhat more badly affected by the blast—much of his left side was burned and I had taken a number of two-inch splinters out of his flesh. I wasn't wholly optimistic about his prospects for recovery.

We had recovered Charles' body, but the only Verheyden who had actually lived through the attack was Christian. He had had the good fortune to be thrown overboard—deliberately—before the explosion. He had been cut about the arms by flying timber and slightly concussed, but had managed to stay conscious long enough to secure a piece of wreckage which kept him afloat. No one had seen what had happened to Jan. Piet had been blown apart by the explosion on the *New Hope's* bridge.

Apart from a few damaged limbs and minor flesh wounds, Al'ha still had a functioning crew. Only two of the Ore'l had actually been killed, and at least one had been shot dead boarding the *New Hope*. That seemed to me like extremely good luck—we could easily have lost six or seven.

The first person I called to see was Thayer, but all I could do was look at him. Conditions weren't exactly ideal for tending a man so badly wounded, and his fate was decidedly in the lap of the gods. He wasn't conscious.

Malpighi, however, was in full possesion of what might charitably be described as his faculties. When I checked his burns he complained that I hadn't set his leg properly.

"I was a bit seasick at the time," I said, not exactly oozing sympathy. (The leg *was* set properly.)

"It hurts," he observed.

"You'll walk again," I assured him. "Though where to, I'm not sure."

"What's going to happen?"

I shrugged.

"Look," he said, "I was against it. Leaving you like that. I didn't want to do it. But I had to string along or they'd have dumped me too. It was me stopped them killing you. And I didn't want to attack your ship, either. When I realized there were humans aboard I begged him to lay off, but that crazy Ogburn. . . ."

"All this," I commented, wearily, "is about as likely as a duck-billed platypus swimming a four-minute mile."

He didn't know what a duck-billed platypus was, but he got the gist of the argument.

"What'll they do?" he asked.

"Not up to me," I commented. "If it was, I'd put on a trial. A big show trial. You know, rather like a circus. I'd try you for crimes against humanity and the Ore'l. Human and alien witnesses, human and alien judges. A nice joint project to symbolize a new era of friendship and cooperation. Ritualize the spirit of unity and all that. I'd sentence you to the maximum possible term of extremely hard labor. The Ore'l will probably want a death penalty, though. They're not as squeamish as I am."

He was scared. He was almost as angry as he was frightened, but there wasn't a lot he could do about it.

"Until then," I said. "I'll look after you. It would be a pity if there were no one left to put on trial."

After that, I went to see Christian. Mariel was in his cabin playing the ministering angel. He didn't have any injuries worth looking at so I just sat down on the edge of the bunk and looked at him in my best bedside manner.

"Tough day," I said, tiredly.

"Yeah," he drawled. He looked pained and listless. In the space of twenty-four hours he had lost a family, and in a rather untidy manner. I suspected that he had always cared about them a lot more than they had cared about him. After all, he was the minority trying to win acceptance and approval. He'd also lost a part-share in an empire, but I don't think that bothered him much. Maybe he was remembering that the last words he'd exchanged with his brothers had been leading up to a fight.

"It's all finished now," I said gently. "*Really* finished. Take it easy for now. In time, you'll pick up the pieces."

His dark eyes stared at me from beneath the brows that had nothing of the Verheyden mold.

"They were right, weren't they?" he said. "You certainly brought a wind of change into our affairs. Is it really over now, or do I go, too."

"They were right," I admitted. "I didn't know how right. I was sure as hell booked to play nemesis. But it *is* over."

"What happened?" he asked.

I glanced at Mariel. She hadn't told him and she shook her head to say so. Maybe she didn't know—she hadn't been in a position to see because I'd been so busy shoving her out of the way.

"Ogburn was just about to start throwing dynamite at *Ilah'y'su,*" I said. "He should have known better. One of Y'su's messengers got there first. It was Piet. Unfortunately, the dynamite was still lit. It went up on the wrong ship. Al'ha says that he saw a thunderbolt come down from heaven to guide Piet's hand. Myself, I think it was the sunlight reflected off the blade—but you never can tell, can you?"

"Did Piet know he was saving your life?" asked Christian.

"What do you think?" I countered.

If Piet had realized what was happening . . . maybe Ogburn would have got to make his throw. We both knew that. And maybe it only *looked* like sunlight flashing from the blade. . . .

172

"So now I inherit the whole thing," said Christian, curling his lip as he said it. "The youngest. The bastard. But the legacy's all mine."

"The legacy's the empire's," I said. "For better or for worse. You'll have to start from scratch. But you're as good as Verheyden. Just do what you can."

"You do it," he said. "You're the one who knows it all. You're the one who blasted apart the old regime. If ever there was ilah'y'su it's surely you. Out of the sky, with the gift of curing and trailing death wherever you go. *You* take over where my mother's husband left off."

"It's your world, Christian," I said.

And I left it at that.

Next, I went to see the animals that were carrying my plague parasites across the ocean for me. They didn't look too well either. But they were only seasick.

I met Mariel in the corridor as I went back to my cabin.

I smiled, faintly. "Plain sailing from now on," I said. "Good ship, fair wind . . . all that crap."

"He'll be all right," she said. "In a few days."

"Sure," I affirmed. "Sea air'll do him a world of good. And with the others all gone . . . he always was the one good bet."

It was a rather cruel judgment—not much of an epitaph for poor Charles and Jan.

"I'll look after him," she said, calmly.

"I know," I replied.

"I'm not even afraid," she said. "You know that crazy feeling . . . all the crazy feelings . . . about losing my power. I'm not afraid now. I don't know why. Maybe all that fighting anaesthetized me. But I can feel for Christian, and somehow I don't think—not any more—that the feeling's being ripped out of my talent. You know what I mean?"

"I understand," I said.

She looked at me, searching my eyes for the answer to an unspoken question. I really didn't have it—not clearly enough to put into a readable thought.

"It's just a matter of balance," I told her. "Find an equilibrium . . . and keep it."

Recommended for Star Warriors!

The Dorsai Novels of Gordon R. Dickson

☐ DORSAI! (#UE1342—$1.75)
☐ SOLDIER, ASK NOT (#UE1339—$1.75)
☐ TACTICS OF MISTAKE (#UW1279—$1.50)
☐ NECROMANCER (#UE1353—$1.75)

The Commodore Grimes Novels of
A. Bertram Chandler

☐ THE BIG BLACK MARK (#UW1355—$1.50)
☐ THE WAY BACK (#UW1352—$1.50)
☐ STAR COURIER (#UY1292—$1.25)
☐ TO KEEP THE SHIP (#UE1385—$1.75)

The Dumarest of Terra Novels of E. C. Tubb

☐ JACK OF SWORDS (#UY1239—$1.25)
☐ SPECTRUM OF A FORGOTTEN SUN (#UY1265—$1.25)
☐ HAVEN OF DARKNESS (#UY1299—$1.25)
☐ PRISON OF NIGHT (#UW1364—$1.50)
☐ INCIDENT ON ATH (#UW1389—$1.50)
☐ THE QUILLIAN SECTOR (#UW1426—$1.50)

The Daedalus Novels of Brian M. Stableford

☐ THE FLORIANS (#UY1255—$1.25)
☐ CRITICAL THRESHOLD (#UY1282—$1.25)
☐ WILDEBLOOD'S EMPIRE (#UW1331—$1.50)
☐ THE CITY OF THE SUN (#UW1377—$1.50)

If you wish to order these titles,
please see the coupon in
the back of this book.

If you wish to order these titles,
please see the coupon in
the back of this book.

If you *really* want to read the best . . .

☐ **WYST: ALASTOR 1716 by Jack Vance.** What was going wrong in this self-advertised Utopian metropolis? A new novel by a Hugo-winning author. (#UJ1413—$1.95)

☐ **Z-STING by Ian Wallace.** After a hundred years, the peace system began to promote war! And they had to cross the Solar System to get at the answer. (#UJ1408—$1.95)

☐ **PURSUIT OF THE SCREAMER by Ansen Dibell.** When the Deathless One awakes, the alarm goes out across a frightened world. (#UJ1386—$1.95)

☐ **CAMELOT IN ORBIT by Arthur H. Landis.** Magic and superscience do not mix, except near Betelguise—and the cause of this has to be solved. (#UE1417—$1.75)

☐ **EARTH FACTOR X by A. E. van Vogt.** The invaders knew all about Earth—except for the little matter of half the human race. (#UW1412—$1.50)

☐ **TOTAL ECLIPSE by John Brunner.** Sigma Draconis—was it a warning of things to come for Sol III? (#UW1398—$1.50)

☐ **STAR WINDS by Barrington J. Bayley.** They sailed the cosmic seas by means of etheric silk—and sheer courage. (#UE1384—$1.75)

DAW BOOKS are represented by the publishers of Signet and Mentor Books, **THE NEW AMERICAN LIBRARY, INC.**

THE NEW AMERICAN LIBRARY. INC.,
P.O. Box 999, Bergenfield, New Jersey 07621

Please send me the DAW BOOKS I have checked above. I am enclosing
$_____ (check or money order—no currency or C.O.D.'s).
Please include the list price plus 35¢ per copy to cover handling costs.

Name _____

Address _____

City _____ State _____ Zip Code _____
Please allow at least 4 weeks for delivery